Assembling Ailish

Assembling Ailish

A Novel

Sharon Guard

POOLBEG

Published 2025 by Poolbeg Press Ltd.
123 Grange Hill, Baldoyle,
Dublin 13, Ireland
Email: poolbeg@poolbeg.com

A catalogue record for this book is available from the British Library.

ISBN 978-1-78199-677-5

www.poolbeg.com

Printed by L&C Printing Group, Poland.

About the Author

Sharon Guard was born in Dublin in 1968, where she still lives and works in the pharmaceutical industry.

She graduated with an MA in Creative Writing from the University of Limerick in 2023. Her short stories and poetry have appeared in New Irish Writing, SWERVE Magazine, The Ogham Stone and the Washing Windows anthologies. She won the Molly Keane Creative Writing Award in 2020 and her story, *Artifice*, was shortlisted for the RTÉ Short Story Competition 2024. *Assembling Ailish* is her first novel.

For Jonathan

She hesitates. She who is told not to break, who is asked
did she break or why did she break.
Go for it, I tell her.

TEACHING MY DAUGHTER HOW TO BREAK AN
EGG
Victoria Kennefick

egg / shell
Carcanet Press (2024)

'Shall we begin?' the woman says.

'Where do we start?'

'There's no right or wrong place. Somewhere that feels natural.'

'A random memory?'

'Specifics are better.'

'From my childhood? Or more recent?'

'Something clear. Something calling.'

You pick up the water.

Sip.

'That's the problem, isn't it?' you say.

'The problem?'

'They're all clear. They're all calling.'

'How do you mean?'

'Everything has equal weight. Equal pull. Now she's gone. There's no new version to figure out, to argue with. To fix. The memories are set. In aspic.'

'Not in aspic.'

'I can't change them.'

Your voice in your ears sounds small. Weak. Pathetic.

'You can change your perspective on them,' the woman says.

'A story I can live with?'

'Isn't that why you're here?'

'I suppose it is.'

A rush of adrenaline – you might have predicted it – catches you unawares.

* * *

My mother was a small-boned woman. Raptor-like, with fluttery hands ...

'What? You said I couldn't get it wrong?'

'It's not wrong. Nothing is wrong,' the woman says. 'Maybe just go in at an actual point in time ... imagine you're there, in the moment.'

'In the moment?'

'Yes.'

'You weren't clear about that.'

* * *

I am nine ...

'Specific enough?' you say.

'Perfect. Proceed. I won't interrupt again.'

'Thank you.'

I am nine. I am …

'One thing?' the woman says.

'Yes?'

'Why fix?'

'Fix?'

'You said 'no new version to fix'?'

'Did I?'

'Yes. Why did you feel you had to fix your mother?'

Breathe. Sip. Breathe.

'Because I broke her,' you say.

1

July 1978

I am nine. I am sitting in the back seat of Daddy's Morris Minor, my legs sticky to grooves stitched in cool grey leather. In the front passenger seat, fuzzing my view of the fuel gauge and radio knobs, Mammy's hair is all soft waves and silky sunlight, the result of a hard night in curlers and pins. She's wearing her mauve dress, the one with the short sleeves, and she's chattering on about Mrs Burke taking over the flowers in the church, not doing them right. What Father Cleary said to Mrs Kavanagh about Paddy and his drinking. Brian Murphy's new job with the council. Names flying like we should know them. Her teeth in side view are spotted with loose flecks of lipstick. Hot Pink. I don't like pink. I don't know why. Most girls my age like pink. My favourite colour is blue.

Daddy doesn't want to be here. Doesn't want to go to Tullamore. I don't know how I know this, but I do. We both know it, in the way we both know how much it annoys Mammy when he tunes the radio to *Music for Middlebrows*, turns it up loud.

'Ah Frank, I can't hear myself think.'

'Maybe you don't have to think for a while, Barbara. Or rabbit on.'

She's driving him mad with all her cackle. He'll say this to me sometimes. 'She drives me mad with all her cackle.' And I don't know what to do when he says this, so I smile and distract him, comb his hair while he's sitting reading the paper, the Brylcreem shiny in slimy strands. Or help him tie his tie in a Windsor knot, the way he showed me. Make him play Snap or Old Maid, tell jokes and do handstands and pull silly faces. Anything to see him smile.

Daddy is handsome. People often say it. His brown hair is neat and slick, cut sharp above the top of his shirt collar, his suit jacket. The skin on the back of his neck is smooth. I think this has to do with him working in an office. It's quite different to Uncle Brendan's neck, which is sweaty and dirty from the farm. I could watch Uncle Brendan's neck for hours, brown splitting to white in the folds. Huge pores, thick with blackheads. I tried to draw them once, the neck and the folds and the blackheads. Miss McEvoy says I've a gift for art. But Mammy didn't like it.

'Oh Ailish, you're such a *perverse* little child,' she said.

I looked it up in our Collins English dictionary:

Perverse: wilfully determined to go against what is expected or desired; contrary.

Daddy said he thought my drawing was interesting, patted me on the head and told me I have a 'unique view of the world', which I prefer. Miss McEvoy sometimes calls Martina Cusack *contrary*. It's not a good thing.

Unique or perverse or even contrary, Uncle Brendan's blackheads are the kind of thing nine-year-old me notices. I like things about people that don't seem to fit. Like Mrs Dunne-next-door's red high heels, which she sometimes wears out on Sundays. She calls them her 'Rita Hayworths'. Or Mr O'Brien's gas mask, which looks like it came from a horror film. He keeps it high up on a shelf in the sitting room. It stares at us when we play. Or Nuala Scanlan's mother's gold tooth, her gum around it gone black, scary when she smiles.

I draw or write notes about things like this in my diary. It came from Santy. I'm suspicious of his existence now, but I love the soft leathery cover, the yellow lined pages, the lock. Daddy told me it was my private space, for my private thoughts, which would be important if I was in boarding school.

I daydream constantly of boarding school. Dormitories and sticky toffee puddings and midnight feasts. Bells for lessons and lacrosse and mean-girl cliques. Feed my imaginings with The Four Marys, St Clare's, Malory Towers.

When I mention such things to Mammy she says:

'Boarding school isn't for people like us, Ailish.'

Which, of course, prompts me to ask: 'What sort of people are we?'

* * *

My National School is only yards up the road from our house, a place of grey-brown brick and tarmacadam. Formica tables, plastic chairs, and tiled floors. Shivery on wintry mornings. The girls who go there aren't called Felicity or Alicia or Gwendolyn. They have names like Sharon, Nicola and Jackie. I think these girls must be 'people like us', but I don't feel I have much in common with them. I overheard my mother say to Mrs Dunne I find it hard to make friends because I'm an only child.

'A lonely child,' Mrs Dunne said.

'Little Miss Speccy Four Eyes, head stuck in a book,' they tease at school.

But mostly they ignore me.

Before I daydreamt of boarding school, before I dreamt of anything, it seemed, I dreamt of a sibling. A little brother, though I would have taken either. An older sister, though I know it's impossible, would be perfect. The O'Brien sisters are a year apart in age. I play with them sometimes. Mrs O'Brien is round and rosy and kind. She bakes fairy cakes with coloured icing and lets us sprinkle Hundreds and Thousands on them. The Girls do everything together. They share a room. I've slept over twice. They brush their teeth for exactly three minutes, wash their faces clockwise, kneel and say prayers before they go to bed. Instead of sheets and bedspreads, they have *duvets* with forget-me-not patterned covers. I got to sleep on a blow-up bed on the floor, which you'd think would be fun, but is kind of uncomfortable.

There was to be a baby once. Properly announced, Mammy's stomach large and round, smiles and excitement and 'Can you feel him kicking?'. One day I came home from school and Mammy wasn't there, was in the hospital. 'I'm sorry Ailish, no baby anymore,' Daddy said, and when Mammy returned she looked smaller, flat. Her hands sitting still on her lap, her dressing gown dirty, her face sad.

I was sent out to play. Was sent to the O'Briens. Buried my head in a book. Mammy's stomach never grew so big again, but there were whisperings. I could see it: a light on, a light off. As if she was there, and then missing.

'Can you not play with me?' I said.

But I must have said it quietly, because Mammy didn't hear. If I had a brother or a sister, we'd be four, a proper family. We might all play together. On my own, only child, lonely child, we're not enough.

Some days, Daddy goes to work and Mammy stays in bed, curtains closed. She smokes in bed. Orla Gaffney said her uncle burned his house down smoking in bed, so I keep check on her. The house smells musty. I open the windows downstairs in the summer, the way Mrs O'Brien does, and sometimes I make my own lunch. I'm good at cooking. Toast and fish fingers is my favourite. When I make Mammy a cup of tea, she cries, tells me I'm a 'grand girl, really'. Once, she gave me a hug. She doesn't hug much. Daddy says some people don't.

＊　＊　＊

In the back of the car now the seats are hot to touch, the July day sizzling through the windowpanes. Hedges fly past, varying shades of green, beyond them fields dotted with cows and horses and donkeys. A smell Uncle Brendan calls 'good clean country air'. It reminds me of the day the drains were blocked in school.

The roads narrow as we near the farm. Mammy wants to pull a window down, Daddy wants it up. I say I want it up too, but I'm starting to feel sick from the heat and the stink. It's hard to breathe. My face is red and the bridge of my glasses is slippery on my nose. My stomach flips and turns and something has turned sour between my parents too.

'You could make an effort,' Mammy says.

'What are you on about now?'

'You could talk to me, talk to the child, try to be cheerful. Make an effort, Frank. We're going on holiday.'

'We're going to your mother's. Your brother's. It's Tullamore. We go there all the time. We have different definitions of a holiday, Barbara.'

'You're determined to ruin it.'

'What do you expect me to do – jump around like a gobshite? Sing nursery rhymes? Ailish is too old for that rubbish now.'

He and I catch each other's eye in the rear-view mirror and he smiles. I have his eyes, cornflower-blue Mammy calls them, a patch of colour in my pale freckle-face. I smile back, my stomach clenched. Knowing that 'gobshite' was like a slap to Mammy because she hates cursing. Hates it when Daddy sometimes does it in front of the neighbours. In front of the cousins. And I don't want to have to take sides. I want this to stop now. I want to be rid of this feeling, creeping like a rash on my skin. I know how they look at us when we arrive at the farm with a row going on. A weakness on us they can smell as we walk through the door.

* * *

Uncle Brendan is Mammy's younger brother, and he and Daddy are about as different as two men can get. Both are tall with brown-blonde hair, but Uncle Brendan is darker-skinned, thickset, solid limbs and a barrel chest. He wears overalls, or cords heavy with grime, and his boots are so caked in mud it is impossible to tell if they were originally brown or black. He smells of manure, even when he has had a bath.

By way of contrast, Daddy is tall and spare. Old Spice clean. He wears suits at the weekend and on holidays. Even gardening, he wears a button-up shirt, his tie removed only for safety. He works in the Civil Service, Mammy tells people. And I don't really know what this means, but her tone implies that it must be terribly important, so I mimic her proudly.

'My daddy works in the Civil Service.'

It doesn't make me more popular.

In my opinion, in Mammy's opinion, Daddy is a proper gentleman compared to the 'rough cut' of Uncle Brendan. Auntie Elena appears to agree. Auntie Elena is Spanish, exotic, impossibly pretty. I could watch her all day. When we arrive, she hugs and kisses Daddy on both cheeks, though nobody in Ireland does this yet. He turns pink in her presence.

'Frank, darling, you must be exhausted. Would you like a coffee?' she says.

Nobody in Ireland calls each other *darling* yet either. Definitely not in Tullamore. And coffee is a continental novelty, a specific bitter-burnt smell, the moka pot on the stove, a foreignness I will forever associate with Auntie Elena. And I'm not looking at her, deliberately not looking at her, but I can feel Mammy bristle, disapproval filling the room. I know if I do look, her face will be set in an expression I associate with danger.

'Ah, maybe just one cup, Elena. You know how the stuff sets me off,' Daddy says.

His voice is different now. Softer. Every syllable carefully pronounced. Auntie Elena giggles, as if he has said something hilarious.

Mammy moves to leave the kitchen but she cuts her turn too sharply on her new black kitten heels, lurches, recovers.

'I'm just going to check on my mother.'

I follow her heavy steps up the rickety dark stairwell. My granny is what they call 'bedridden', has been for as long as I can remember. Nobody is quite sure what the matter is. They say she can walk, could dress herself, could even do light chores, but she doesn't.

'I'm seventy-five. Sure didn't I do enough?'

Seventy-five seems impossibly old when you're not even ten yet, so all I can do is nod in agreement.

'Raised my own two, raised Brendan's three. All those years, Ailish. Running the farm with Peter. It was a hard life, you know.'

Her hips are banjaxed, she tells me. Her knees are worse. I overhear the adults say she's going senile.

'What's senile, Granny?' I say.

'It's when you finally get the bit of rest you deserve.'

Her room smells of Nivea and wee and Ritchie's Original

After Dinner Mints. With a wrinkled wink, she slips me a half-full bag, and I curl up on the bedspread beside her fluid form, stomach and breasts melting into my skinny limbs like a warm candlewick cushion.

'How's that young Ruth Molloy? Is she still giving you grief over your specs?'

'I think she's forgotten about me, Granny.'

'Found another target?'

'Brenda Doyle has braces now. And glasses.'

'Did you get the Deep Heat?' she asks Mammy.

'I got you some last time,' Mammy says.

'Ah sure, I'm out of that since last week. You know how I go through it. My back is a trial.'

'Can Elena not get you some?'

'I don't like to ask.'

'You don't mind asking me.'

'Well, that's because you're my daughter. It's different.'

Granny has a different voice when she talks to Mammy. I've noticed it before. Scratchy, grating. Disgruntled. As if she is always trying to control the cross remark. Sometimes she can't.

'That skirt is too short on you,' she says.

'It's only above the knee.'

'You're too old for it.'

'It's the fashion. Everyone is wearing them.'

'You're forty-two.'

'I know that.'

'Not a young one.'

'I know that too.'

There's a kettle on a sideboard squeezed in under the window. My mother takes it and goes downstairs to fill it. Granny opens a drawer in her bedside locker and pulls out a *Misty* comic, hands it to me. There's a tiny plastic bag stuck on the front and in it a replica of a ring characters wear when they're inducted into 'The Cult of the Cat', one of the series stories. It's gold and black, a flat disc embossed with the shape of an Egyptian cat. It is possibly the most glamorous thing I have ever seen.

'*Shhh*, now,' Granny says, eyes glinting with mischief.

Auntie Elena buys comics for Granny to give to us grandchildren when she's doing her weekly shop. There's always a stash. I love *Misty*, but Mammy says it's too advanced for me, too spooky, will give me nightmares. And it does.

'Go, run and hide it in your room,' Granny says.

And I do, picking the ring out of the packet greedily as I run.

When I come back, Mammy is kneeling on the floor, gently lifting Granny's feet – left one, right one – into a basin of soapy water to soak. It's toenail day. I curl up on the crumpled sheets of the bed, grab a pillow, help myself to another mint, run the pad of my thumb over the ring, hidden now in my shorts pocket. Watch intently. The hardened yellow nails, the crickle-cracked skin. The softening, the clipping, the patting dry. The Scholl foot cream. The dance between the two women.

'Aaah, don't chop my toe off, Barbara.'

'Sit still, would you?'

'I'm hardly running off down the road, am I?'

Everybody says they're close, but I'm not so sure about that.

* * *

Auntie Elena appears with a tray of tea and sandwiches for her mother-in-law and entreats us downstairs. It's half past three and my cousins will be home from school soon.

The adults gather around the pine table, high with coffee and tea and cake and sandwiches piled on colourful Spanish plates. The kitchen is dark, even on sunny days. My parents sit beside each other, guarded, avoiding eye contact, the row in the car still festering. Auntie Elena fusses while Uncle Brendan pads stocking feet on cracked lino, washes his hands in the big white sink, a fluorescent green squirt of Fairy Liquid, the muck from his hands soiling the white bottle, the cartoon baby. Auntie Elena shrieks and swats him with her tea towel. They laugh. He announces that he has finished fixing the fence in the top field and is going to leave the milking to Ned.

'Is Ned still here?' Mammy says. 'I thought you'd got rid of him?'

'The man can do what he likes with his labourers, Barbara,' Daddy says.

'I didn't say he couldn't, Frank, but Ned is a halfwit. He left the gate to the top field open – we could have lost most of the herd. And it's not the first time.'

'Decent labourers are hard to get at the moment, Barb,' Uncle Brendan says. 'They're all heading to Dublin, and the ones that are here are looking for an arm and a leg for a day's work.'

'Well, you get what you pay for. That man could have cost us a fortune.'

Daddy looks cross. Cross with the conversation. Cross with Mammy. Uncle Brendan lives on the farm, will inherit the farm when Granny dies, even I know this, but Mammy doesn't think he's looking after it properly. She says this. A lot. Daddy tells her it's none of her business and it always causes a row.

'Don't worry, Ailish,' Auntie Elena says, ruffling my hair. 'All this adult talk. The children will be home soon. You can go play with your cousins. They're so looking forward to seeing you.'

I doubt this is true, and the thought of them being ordered to play with me fills me with dread.

* * *

My cousins are farm children. Robust. A certain boldness expected, tolerated. And they are half-Spanish, which is excuse enough in itself, their wildness greeted cheerfully by adults smitten with their dark eyes, tanned skin, their zest for mischief. When they descend features soften, lips curl into smiles. The air itself fizzes with life and promise and fun.

I hover by my mother, pick at the sleeve of her dress. My hand is compelled by a mock pocket sitting on her right breast, my fingers landing softly, earning a swift swat and: '*Ailish*, what on earth is the matter with you?' Her voice high and shrill.

All eyes on me now, glasses sliding down my freckled nose in a sweat. My face aflame. Auntie Elena unfurls from her youngest, Louisa, rises to take charge.

'Come on, you guys, time to go play. You should be outside on a day like this. There are so few of them in Ireland.'

She smiles at Daddy, who is chatting to Joe about football, about Georgie Best going to the United States. A language I don't understand. A language my father speaks with passion, his face alive in the conversation. I wish I had a brother. No, I wish I was a boy. I wish I was a boy, and I wish Mammy was fun like Auntie Elena, and Daddy would always be as he is now, carefree and full of football, without the worry of Mammy. Without the worry of me.

My stomach is hard now, like it is made of stone. I slip the cat ring onto my finger, turn it into my palm, will its magic properties to seep into my skin. Make me a witch. Give me the power to cast spells. The power to make everything better. Although if you were to ask me, I don't think I would be able to tell you what is wrong. Maybe I would simply say: everything.

'How are you today?'

You shrug.

'It was a busy week,'

You shift in the seat.

'Lots going on.'

'Work?'

'Work. Home. Saoirse's back from London. Róisín's mooching about. Her boyfriend is there. The house is busy.'

'Good busy? Bad busy?'

'Busy, busy. There's a Mass on Saturday.'

And from a quietly composed moment, you are now weeping, the words caught on a whimper.

'It's her anniversary?'

'The first.'

'A full Mass?'

'Yes. And a gathering.'

'That's a lot to take on.'

You blow your nose. Shake yourself.

'She'd expect it. The extended family expect it. The neighbours expect it.'

'How do you feel about it?'

'Well …'

Breathe.

'It's all about the show, isn't it?' you say. 'It goes on. Regardless.'

You look away from the woman's face, towards the heater, towards the table. Take a tissue.

2

The cousins take me cow-tipping. At least, this is what they tell me we are doing. Cows horrify me. Something about their calm, their filmy fathomless eyes. The solidness of them. Their hooves. It's a weakness I try to keep to myself. I feel like an annoying little tag-along. I *am* an annoying little tag-along. Two years younger than Louisa, who is a year younger than Sarah, who is a year younger than Joe. A four-year gap top-to-bottom must seem like nothing to the adults, but to me thirteen-year-old Joe seems almost an adult himself. The girls have their mother's grace and style, their cut-off-jeans trendy, their tops blousy and foreign against my stripy Dunnes T-shirt and shorts. Louisa's hair is straight and bobbed. Sarah's is a mass of wavy curls, a random few strands plaited and tied with a tiny bow, which looks cool. When my hair grows a bit, I resolve to try something similar.

We trek through dried-out fields, sparse grass and crusty cowpats. I watch my new runners – white rubber against pink canvas – sidestep danger, the sun beating down on the back of my neck where my hair parts, my arms, my legs. I can feel the burn already. Anticipate the redness, the tight and peeling skin.

'All right, Ailish?' Sarah says.

I nod.

'What class are you going into now?' Louisa says, though she knows this, must know this. I am always two years behind her.

'Fourth,' I say.

'Sarah's starting with the nuns in September. Sister Bríd is fierce, they say. Marie Devlin is terrified of her. Mama says they'll put manners on our Sarah.'

Sarah swipes at her sister playfully. She's pulling dandelion puffballs, blowing seeds to a cloudless blue sky, her fingers stained brown in spots with sap.

'I'll take no messing from those nuns, I tell you,' she says. 'Concepta Murphy says they're all just a shower of Mickey-dodgers.'

They laugh. The sort of laugh Mammy would call a dirty laugh. I don't understand, but I blush. I blush a lot when I'm with my cousins. Sarah, in particular, confuses me. While Joe and Louisa largely ignore or tease me about my 'Dublin ways', Sarah is sometimes kind. Occasionally she will share her sweets or step in with an 'Ah, leave her be' when they get carried away.

And really now, I don't trust even Sarah anymore. Can't. Not since Halloween. Not since the night of the ghosts. No cat ring to protect me then.

* * *

At Halloween we'd had a break from school. Mammy was keen to go down home, Daddy less so. They'd been bickering about it, a row that ended in days of 'Ailish, tell your mammy this', 'Ailish, tell your daddy that'. Mammy excited about something, then upset, then cross, with everything, with me, for some reason I don't understand.

'She needs to go out and play, she's been stuck to me all day,' she says.

Her voice is high, her cheeks sharp and veiny without make-up.

'I'm beyond exhausted with her,' she says.

I don't want to leave her and I don't want to go play with the O'Briens. They're in a snippy mood too, and there are no other neighbours my age around. I've refused a game of chasing, some other sin, and now I'm No-Fun-Ailish. Tired of being the outsider. Battling two to one for things I want to do. Plus the weather is cold. I don't feel well. I whinge. I moan. I want to stay in the warm kitchen, I want to shrink right back to a baby, crawl onto Mammy's lap, curl into the folds of her fluffy Angora jumper. Smell her perfume. Touch her hair, stiff with spray.

I don't heed the warning signs. I pick at the woollen pleats of her skirt, beg to watch television, beg for a Fig Roll, beg for attention. I'm fidgety and awkward and mobile and I twist and turn and fall, topple into her, land full force on the small bones of her foot. She screams. The fright of it. She's upright in a millisecond, hands beating like frantic bird-wings, landing on my shoulders, my arms, my back, my face. Knocking my glasses to the floor. Her engagement ring catches the side of my eye and I howl.

'Jesus Christ, Barbara, leave the child alone. You lunatic!'

Daddy pulls her off me, grabs one of her arms tight. Grabs the other one. They tussle, arms and legs twitching. A parent monster. Then an extraordinary thing. She starts to cry. Softly at first, tears rising, breaking, sobbing, heaving like I do when I'm upset, and he holds her, he holds her, and he croons and he kisses the top of her head and tells her everything will be all right, Bar, and she says she is sorry, she is so, so sorry, that she doesn't want things to be this way, and he says he knows she doesn't. He knows she doesn't. He says it's okay, she can go down home and it will be fine, it will all be fine.

After the longest time, they part, remember me. Daddy ruffles my hair, bends, picks up my broken glasses.

'It's all right, pet,' he says.

Mammy, her face puffed, heaves a sob, her shoulders shaking. Stops with effort. Blows her nose.

'Come on Ailish, let's get ready,' she says. 'You'll have a grand time playing with your cousins.'

As if nothing has happened.

* * *

A phone call may have been made, but it feels like we weren't expected. Uncle Brendan is out somewhere in the fields with Joe. Daddy announces he'll go for a walk, see if he can see them and Mammy goes upstairs to see Granny.

Auntie Elena is in flight, full of dress-up and hanging decorations and talk of apple-bobbing fun with the girls.

'In Spain, this time of year is a big thing, Ailish. We call Halloween *Día de las Brujas*, Day of the Witches. The girls and I have been putting our costumes together. Shall we see if we can make a fabulous witch out of you too? Would you like that?'

Scrunching down, she puts her arm around me kindly. I nod, conscious of the mark at the side of my eye, the scratch and bulge of it begging explanation. I say: 'I fell off the bed.' Auntie Elena doesn't say anything. Squeezes my shoulder. Two pulses. Kisses the top of my head.

She supervises lightly while the girls pull random clothes from the dress-up box, old tops and blouses and floaty slip nighties that make me uneasy when I think of them on a grown woman. On Auntie Elena. Not garments I could ever imagine my mother in. They produce a black adult T-shirt, long sleeves and a scooped neck, fasten it onto me with a rope belt, tuck and roll. Sarah cuts stars from a sheet of glittered paper and sticks them on with glue. We make pointy black cardboard hats, draw and colour shapes on them with pastels at the big kitchen table, while Auntie Elena fusses with dinner preparations. I grow almost relaxed. Almost comfortable.

* * *

An elderly neighbour has died and is being waked in his house half a mile away. His son is a local councillor, the family well got. The adults decide to go pay their respects together after dinner, leaving us children alone in the house with Granny, almost absent, but still an adult. Strong warnings about bedtime. It is something they sometimes do, leave us like this, and I don't like it. It always leads to what Mammy calls 'hijinks'. Me being teased.

Tonight, Joe, always eager for an audience and fuelled now with sugar, is in the mood for scary storytelling. He's stalking through the house in a purple cape Auntie Elena made from an old velvet curtain, a plastic top hat and Dracula fangs. He gathers us up, turns the top lights off in the sitting room and commands us to sit. I sink into worn sofa cushions, bockety springs sticking sideways into my bum. My legs and feet raised. Escape difficult.

His face is up-lit by a lamp from a side-table placed on the floor in front of him. With slow *woo woo* sounds and gestures, he tells us the story of a girl, who lived in this house, many, many years ago. Her name was Mary and she was blonde and pretty, an orphan being reared by her uncle, who had promised her hand in marriage to a neighbouring farmer when she turned eighteen. If she married this man – who was old and wrinkled, fat and covered in warts – her uncle would be able to join the two farms together and become rich. However, when Mary was seventeen, she fell in love with Patrick, a handsome farmhand, and she became pregnant.

'When her uncle found out, he flew into a rage, beat her with a poker until her brains where splattered all over this *very room, this very floor, this very fireplace …*' Joe says, his arms waving the cape dramatically for effect.

The girls *oooh* and *aaah*.

I say nothing.

'She's forever trapped now within these walls, and her spirit walks our hallways *every Halloween*, lamenting her *unborn baby*.'

The story makes me uncomfortable. I don't think Uncle Brendan and Auntie Elena would approve. Mammy and Daddy definitely wouldn't.

The girls cheer. Joe takes a bow.

Strains of *The Late Late Show* opening credits snake their way through the house from Granny's bedroom. She watches it on the portable TV in her room. I think she is in love with Gay Byrne. She bangs on the floor, shouts at us to wrap it up, go to bed, and we dutifully tidy away evidence of the play.

* * *

I'm exhausted by the time I open the door to my bedroom. Close it gratefully, click it shut. Wonder could I, should I, turn the key in the brass lock with the pretty patterned doorknob. Stare at it. Turn the key. Slowly. Quietly. To avoid alerting cousins or ghosts. The lock is loose and it shakes and rattles. A soft breeze from somewhere is whooshing under the door. But I am brave, I tell myself. I am not spooked.

My bag is on the bed, a Bay City Rollers tote, given to me for Christmas by Auntie Elena. A cool alternative to the Dunnes bag supplied by my mother. I take out my pyjamas, toothbrush, toothpaste.

In summer, this room feels like a haven. The standalone sink in the corner with the splashback and glass and toothbrush holders somehow terribly grown-up. I'm too short yet to see myself in the mirror, but I could look out the windows either side all day, watch the activity in the yard, tractors and dogs and cats and Uncle Brendan herding cows towards the milking parlour. Though I am no huge fan of rolling fields and cattle, in summer even I can see the beauty.

In winter, though, this room feels bleak. Chilly. I should go for a wee, but I don't want to run into the others, so I brush my teeth and wash my face here, bury my nose and lips in the matching facecloth and towel, inhale the familiar scent of Imperial Leather.

I collapse on the bed. Submit to the thin mattress, curl onto my side. Turn off the lamp on the bedside locker. *The Famous Five* can wait. I won't read tonight. I won't sink my face into the pillow. I will wallow in silent turmoil. I won't cry.

The wind is howling behind homemade curtains more suited, I imagine, to Spain. Not lined, not heavy enough to exclude the spiralling whistle. Joe's story is playing in my head, words converting to images I can see clearly. The girl's blonde hair and pretty tear-stained face. The uncle, dark and heavyset. A moustache and a morning coat, like on *Upstairs, Downstairs*. I don't know what might have been involved in getting her pregnant, have no concept of these things, but the humiliation of her, the destruction of her, is real, and it is in this room.

I put my fingers in my ears to shut out the wind. Another low keening. A sound which shoots adrenaline through my veins like needles, my stomach painful with stress, my face, my eyes, my eyelids, frozen from it. A noise which escalates. Comes from outside, from inside, from above. From beneath. The bed moves. The mattress begins to elevate. Me, rigid, terrified, in a slow ascent to flight.

I scream but nothing comes out. The bed rises higher, the keening gets louder. A sound escapes onto the cold dusty air; a sound that isn't human, isn't me, is fractured, in agony. It fills the room, fills the house, fills the world.

I jump. I fly. Launch myself at the doorknob, slippery beneath my palm, the key cutting into my fingers as I pull at it, deranged with fright. Noise behind me. After me.

A scramble from under the bed.

Joe.

Louisa.

Laughing.

A voice from outside, a pull on the doorknob, in the other direction. The door opens. Sarah standing, lovely in her nightdress, tiny daisies picking holes in pure-white cotton against her honey-coloured skin. I fall forward, awkwardly, my head landing hard on her chest, causing her to yelp.

'Ah lads, you've gone too far,' she says. 'Way too far.'

The other two pull themselves upright. Still laughing. I'm still screaming. She puts her arm around my shoulders, her hand clasping my elbow. Pulls me tight.

'It's all right, Ailish, it's all right. *Shush*. Go away you two and leave her alone.'

She guides me towards the bed, hushing and comforting and crooning. My tears fall freely now, staining the front of her nightdress, greying the stitching. I sob. Great heaves. She curls in beside me, spoons me, strokes my hair. Starts to sing: *When you wish upon a star*. I cry more. Deep guttural sounds that come unbidden from some embarrassing, buried place.

'Sorry,' I say.

'*Shush, a leanna,*' she says.

The way Granny might.

'It's all right, everything is okay.'

* * *

Eventually, I doze. Uneasily. After some time, maybe only minutes, I feel her move, quietly pull away, limb by limb, slip from beneath the sheets, tuck them, the quilt, in around my shoulders. I wonder will she kiss my forehead, say goodnight in a soft breath, but she doesn't. She makes her way to the door, the sound of bare feet trying not to make a noise. Tippytoes.

I lie, warm now but stiffening. Can feel my feet growing icy, wish I'd asked Sarah for a hot water bottle. From a semi-asleep state, I am fully conscious. Rain hard on the window. A drip somewhere. Mice scurrying through walls.

I get up. Pad across the threadbare rug, to the door. I don't want to act like a baby. But. I can't stay in this room on my own. I think of Granny on the other side of the house. The best route to get to her. If I run into my cousins, I can tell them I'm on the way to the loo. I turn the handle, crack the door open a sliver. A fraction more. Hear voices. Pull it back to a treacherous earwigging slit.

'For fuck's sake, Joe,' Sarah says.

The swear word, her tone, harsh, zinging like a bullet in the small hallway, explodes, disperses like a gas. Envelops me.

'You're a pure gobshite. Mama will kill us if she goes whinging about this.'

'Oh, shut up, Sarah – it's not like you're always a saint with her,' Joe says. 'She's a pain in the hole, coming down from Dublin thinking she's better than us. Why the fuck are they here again? I thought they weren't coming this weekend?'

'You know how it is, Joe. You're not a baby. Barbara's not right, is she? And she's gone completely mental now. Did you not see the cut on poor Ailish's face? There's weird stuff going on in that family. I feel sorry for her. And Mama will go ballistic if we upset her. Cop yourself on.'

'The extended family is quite big now?'

'Yes. The cousins, their husbands, wives, children. Frank is still here, obviously. And Elena. Brendan passed away two months after Mum.'

'They'll all go to the Mass?'

'A lot of them. Elena will insist.'

'You and Elena get on well?'

'Elena? Oh, Elena and I sorted our differences a long time ago, I think.'

'You had differences?'

You shrug.

'Where is the gathering?' the woman says.

'Our house.'

You want to say 'my house' or 'home', but neither feel accurate.

You would rather say 'hotel'.

'That's a lot to take on.'

'My mother's family, the Mannions, are good at gatherings. The Kennedys too. That's my husband Gerry's family.'

'And your name is McCarthy?'

'I kept my maiden name. My father's surname. We never really have our own, do we?'

'Well, I guess we can choose.'

'I probably always felt more of a Mannion. No, actually, maybe not. But we never did see much of my father's family. They're from Donegal. He was an only child too.'

You realise this is the first time you've considered this. If it is relevant. To anything.

3

September 1981

I stand in line in the assembly hall with the rest of the first-year intake. I am wearing a sky-blue dress, ruched with a tidy white collar, white knee-socks and white leather sandals, scuffed, a loose buckle held by robustly wound thread, at the end of their short summer life now it is September. The only footwear I own apart from runners and the clunky brogues bought to go with my school uniform. It's own-clothes induction day. The others wear drainpipe jeans, chunky knits, T-shirts and denim jackets, thick with button badges. Names of bands I've never heard of. I'm holding the Alice band my mother insisted went so well with the outfit loose in the folds of my skirt, a vain hope the lack of it might help me look more like the others.

My parents are sitting at the back of the hall with the other parents, waiting for the show to begin. Our Lady's is an all-girls fee-paying school and there is, at least on my mother's behalf, an expectation. Exactly of what is unclear to me, but I too am alive with anticipation. I hop from one foot to another, scanning the rows in front and behind for a friendly face, but the girls are already caught in clusters of twos and threes, feeding from each other, confidence growing and rising like an escalating sound-cloud above the room. Deafening.

I can't see anybody I know, apart from Eimear McCormack, who stole my sandwiches on the first day of junior infants, and is now about seven foot tall. I'm sure she still hates me because I cried and got her into trouble. The other girls from primary school have mostly gone to St Catherine's, the non-fee-paying school up the road from our house.

There's a girl wearing a kilt and Aran-type sweater, also with glasses. A wintery version of me. We catch each other's eye and I know immediately we will be friends, and I know she knows it too. We are united now in our classmates' eyes by a severe lack of cool. Her name is Fiona, I will find out later, as our parents drink stewed tea and nibble stale Kimberly biscuits from paper plates. She is brunette and pretty beneath the glasses, pale-blue eyes and skin that will tan if she and I ever escape the half-hearted grey drizzle which coats the long length of the assembly-hall windows.

On a stage bordered with red-velvet curtains, a small flat-faced nun, our principal, Sister John, welcomes us. My fantasies of boarding school fizzle in excitement at the formality of her tone, her steady assurance, but I am distracted by two girls in the queue ahead giggling and pucking at each other. Another nun, heavyset, sweat-beads on her upper lip, curls sneaking wild from her wimple, is patrolling the line. She shushes them.

'Sorry, Sister Bríd,' the blonde one says.

Many of the girls know each other. Many of them came to junior school here. But my parents couldn't justify that sort of money for primary, not when, as my mother tells anybody who will listen, everybody knows National Schools have the best teachers anyway. Paid by the state, jobs that are safe, permanent and pensionable. Though now I am going to Our Lady's, she says things like:

'Well, we only have the one, you know, so we want to give her the best.'

Or:

'Of course, she's completely spoiled. But what can you do?'

And:

'You're so lucky to get this opportunity, Ailish. If we had more children, we wouldn't be able to afford to spend all this money on you.'

She has a job now, as a receptionist in a doctor's surgery, three mornings a week when I am at school, and it suits her. She's put on a little weight, has more colour in her cheeks. She wears modest dresses, Brendella skirts, blouses with pussycat bows. Puts on make-up, pink lipstick, blue eyeshadow. Some days I look at her and think how pretty she must have been when she was younger. Can see it clearly when she smiles.

The back of the hall is full of people, adults and children, the clink-clink of cheap cups and saucers. Daddy is in his element chatting to the nuns, the other mothers, the teachers. I'm not used to seeing him in such a public social setting, working a room, and it makes me squirm. Fiona rustles in her kilt beside me.

'Your daddy is very handsome,' she says.

And though I don't know her well yet, I feel like smacking her.

* * *

The excitement of secondary is muted because two weeks ago we found out Granny has cancer. 'The big C' forms in a whisper on my mother's lips when she tells people, a hopeless, helpless look. She is scared, and it scares me too. She has been through this before, lost a parent. I know him only through stories told by Granny and Mammy and Uncle Brendan, over the dinner table, under the influence of Auntie Elena's wine, or the stout and spirits which appear in our houses at Christmas. The inevitable tears and raised voices.

From the stories and photographs I've pieced together a picture. My grandfather was the size of a giant, six-foot-four, superhuman. Strong and stern, waiting up for my mother with a strap when she stayed out late at a dance. Kind when he showed her how to milk a cow properly. Business-like when he had to castrate a bull, wring the neck of a chicken, because Granny would not, could not. A legend because of how he dealt with his own illness, a stomach cancer there was no painkiller strong enough for, tales of him biting on a wooden dowel to stay his screams, tales of broken teeth. A horse, Billy, his favourite, who mourned him with actual tears as he left the house for the final time in his coffin.

When we visit, I realise Granny remembers all this, and more, first hand too. Is terrified. Smaller. Reduced in the bed, stiff in white sheets, with her blue candlewick bedspread packed tight by specialist nurses who visit three times a day, give her medication for the pain.

I pat her hand and she smiles with a weak 'Hey, chicken'.

I'm afraid to do more, to hurt her. I choke back a tear. The thought of her gone is too huge to comprehend.

'Can the doctors not do something?' I say to my mother.

'It's gone to her liver,' she says.

As if I should know what this means. As if I am fully part of, or party to, the horror-mix of upset and whispering going on: she needs to be in hospital, we can't manage the pain here, we have to respect her wishes, it's frightening for the children, they're farm children, they know about life and death, she should be in hospital, we have to respect her wishes, she wants to die here …

She doesn't want to die, here or anywhere else. I know this as I hold her hand, her veins pumping hard beneath her soft smooth skin, the way it gathers in pleats when I press it, slowly unfurls. She presses back. How easily she bruises.

They insist I go back to Dublin with Daddy. My education is expensive. Important. Classes cannot be missed. Mammy and Auntie Elena are to battle out the duties of care. I cry when we go, sitting alongside Daddy in the front of the car, able now to touch the smooth walnut of the dashboard, the knobs and dials, the steering wheel. Strange constants in a world turned weird.

* * *

I sit beside Fiona in almost every class. We have been streamed via an entrance exam, Science and Business, One to Three, six classes in total, and we are in Science One. Though it's never voiced, we are the top stream, the Honours class, the best teachers assigned, the expectations high. She is a little better at Science and Maths, me at English and Art. We almost always achieve As, get competitive in the detail of ninety-three versus ninety-four per cent. Smile sweetly. Congratulate each other.

While on school premises we are equal. Two bespectacled nerds, zoned out by the hip kids, the ones with musical and dramatic talents, the ones who watch *Top of the Pops*, know what's in the charts, wear legwarmers and fingerless gloves. When we go home on the bus, I get off near the entrance to my estate, slip into the unheated beige-and-magnolia flowery folds of our three-bed semi-D, while Fiona stays on for a couple of stops, disembarks at a yellow double-fronted Georgian villa, basement and conservatory, low-lit tassel-shaded lamps, velvet curtains, antiques. When I visit, I am immediately at home here beneath the high ceilings, walls lined with books, thick cracked floorboards and mangy rugs. There's a smell of Tullamore. A whiff of polish, something real and comforting, a familiar air of damp. Fiona has only been to my house a couple of times. Mammy doesn't encourage it and it seems so boring and colourless by comparison.

Fiona is also an only child, but her parents are long separated. Her father lives in France. Her mother, Yvonne, is an artist. She has wild grey-streaked hair and wears floor-length dresses in solid primary colours which dwarf her rather small frame. You can tell she too was once pretty, beneath her habitual puzzled frown, lines etched solid between her eyes as if she is thinking thoughts so deep they have left actual scars. When she smiles, as she does when she sees us, it is almost in surprise, as if a daughter and friend are unexpected. An interruption to some important debate she is conducting in her head. I like her, and I think she likes me, which is also unexpected. She speaks to us as if we are adults already. She says '*fuck*' in a posh accent. Often.

* * *

Granny dies on a Tuesday in January. Daddy is waiting for me after school, standing by the car, talking to one of the other parents. He shakes his head slightly and I know. I climb in. Expected but indigestible news. Everything alien. We go home and I pack a small bag, a black skirt and top Mammy sent us to buy weeks ago, one of her many listed items. We don't speak, but we visit McDonald's on the way. A Big Mac meal and strawberry milkshake, a quarter pounder for Daddy. A treat usually reserved for birthdays.

Since Mammy has been staying with Granny, taken leave from her job, it's been just the two of us in the house. A lot of the time, it's been me alone. He goes to work early and isn't home until after six. Sometimes it's later because he goes to the pub. He doesn't say this. He will tell me he has a meeting to go to, but when he comes in I can smell the smoke, the tang of Guinness, other mingling odours. When I ask to play draughts or cards or Scrabble he'll swerve, have to cut the grass, replace a lightbulb, go to the shops.

He buys the food, and I cook it. Simple stuff. Chops and carrots. Sausages and peas. Fish fingers and beans on Friday.

Always potatoes. Boiled or mashed. Fiona's mum teaches us to cook spaghetti bolognese and I bring some home, but Daddy's not keen on it. He's grumpy a lot. We don't play or joke the way we used to when I was little. If I look for a hug, he shoos me away.

'You're too big for all of that now,' he says.

* * *

Squished amongst my cousins in the funeral car, I'm aware their lengths and breadths are shifting. Even though it's been only weeks since I've seen them, Joe is taller, the girls have sprouted curves. Louisa, still shorter and rounder than Sarah, is given to pulling on her bra-strap often, as if to make a point of it. I feel like a small child beside them, my school coat buttoned and belted. Mammy insisted I wear it. The school badge is a double statement. I go to a private school. I don't own another coat. Sarah and Louisa comment only with their eyes.

Joe walks behind his father towards the church. He looks uncomfortable, waiting for the hearse to unburden itself of the coffin onto brass runners. He's sixteen now and there's an energy about him, something cool and somehow dangerous. Uncle Brendan greets mourners with smiles, and in soft moments looks lost. Hairs stray across his big farmer head, get caught in squally spittle. Auntie Elena, effortless and composed, finds her place with the girls, who are full of chatter.

'I'm going to miss her apple tarts,' Louisa says.

'She hasn't made them for ages,' Sarah says.

'She made them before she was sick.'

'She stopped making them ages ago.'

'I wish I'd known the last one was the last one.'

'I don't. I wouldn't have enjoyed it.'

More like this. Conversations I could contribute to, but I don't. Even the parts I was there for, I feel I wasn't. I am nothing. I am white space. I am a ghost, conjuring images of Granny in the kitchen in her crossover apron, her overalls she called them, wrestling roasts and cakes out of the range; in the garden, when I was little, picking peas, carving my initials – AMcC – in her marrows and watching them grow; her sitting with Nibbles, the old ginger tomcat, on her lap on a dilapidated deck chair in the back yard. She claimed he was more dog than cat, showed me how to stroke his hair the way he liked it. Sometimes I'd catch them in a quiet moment, faces turned towards the sun, the two of them utterly content. I remember how she cried when he died. Mammy saying it was only a cat. Cross with her because she was being 'sentimental'.

'We're only here for a minute, Ailish,' Granny said. More than once. 'This life is a valley of tears. Only preparation for the next one.'

* * *

My mother's sobs penetrate like tiny scalpels now. I can feel them, sharp and real as stabs. But, still, I don't believe it. Cannot believe that Granny has simply gone, though I know she has. That is why I am here, here watching the undertakers, stiff, like constipated crows, steel-sharp hair, dandruff like stardust on their shoulders, shivering when they move. I am here, taking in the tabernacle, tiles and rails and tapestry kneelers, the aftermath of incense. I am here, watching my mother, grief etched in skin stretched shiny on her face. She will miss the softness of her mother, I think. I will miss that softness. I miss that softness.

There's after-funeral food back at the farmhouse. Sandwiches, cheese and ham and corned beef on limp buttered white bread, cling-filmed trays of them brought by neighbours. Apple tarts and jam tarts and Swiss Roll and Fig Rolls and Battenberg and French Fancies. Bowls of Hula Hoops. I hover, pick at them. Some of their neighbours have brought their children, the cousins have some friends of their own here. The house is packed with strangers and half-familiar faces. They talk about my grandmother as if they knew her, which I realise they did.

'If ever a woman was going straight to heaven, it's your mother, Barbara.'

'Even Father Murphy had tears in his eyes. Choked up on that eulogy, he was. He'll miss her terrible, the chats they used to have.'

'Such a devoted woman.'

'Carmel was a good neighbour.'

'She was my oldest friend, Brendan. What am I going to do without her?'

Life has gone on, goes on, in this house when I am not present. Which is not a surprise, yet it is. I slide into a corner beside the Aga, pick at the terracotta-tile lino with my foot, my Christmas shoes, black Mary Janes. My back is slick to exposed brick, a small space to lean into. I lose my footing, right myself. Look up and see a blonde boy, styled in the manner of Nick Hayward from Haircut One Hundred, blue white shirt, floppy fringe, looking at me. Directly.

'You okay?' he says.

His lips are full for boy's lips. Fiona's *Jackie* magazine would call them 'kissable'. I feel as if I have entered the pages, become a character in a photo story. I'm conscious of every part of me. How I'm standing, what I'm wearing. How short I am beside this boy-man.

'Fine,' I say.

Blush. Try not to blush. Blush more.

'Would you like some Fanta? You look a bit pale,' he says.

'I'm grand.'

'I'm Michael. Michael Hegarty, Joe's friend. From up the road.'

His accent is softer than Joe's. Musical. His hand hovers in front of him, as if it wants to reach across the space but, as soon as I realise maybe I should put mine out to shake it, he retrieves it, returns it to his pocket.

'Are you the cousin from Dublin?' he says.

And I suppose I must be, so I nod.

'Ailish.'

'Pleased to meet you, Ailish.'

His eyes are dark blue. He doesn't blink.

'Sorry, for, you know … sorry about your granny. She was a great woman.'

'Thank you.'

I smile. Realise I shouldn't be smiling. Try to look sad. But the sad I couldn't shake a moment ago is nowhere to be found.

'We'll miss her terribly,' I say.

And my voice is formal, posh, South County Dublin. It's changed, I've changed it, not deliberately, but maybe a little, to fit in with the girls at school. It's been noted by the cousins. I've caught the arched eyebrows thrown from one to another. This boy must know about me from them. What sort of stories have they told? But. He smiles.

Joe sidles up.

'C'mon, Hegarty.'

And they depart, Michael following Joe obediently, shirt tucked into jeans, long legs I can't stop looking at. I know they're going out back for a smoke. Auntie Elena won't have it in the house. Joe wouldn't normally do it in front of her at all, but today all rules are flexible.

Left behind in the kitchen, I am tiny, but I feel huge, awkward. As if all the emotion running through me must be pouring out of me. Must be visible. I need to find another space, go seek my mother out. She's in the front room, her eyes puffed and sore-looking, standing by the window, the closed curtains, being comforted by a neighbour, a friend of Granny.

The woman is resting a hand on her shoulder and saying over and over: 'Terrible, poor Carmel. After all she's been through. Terrible. She didn't deserve that, she didn't.'

'What did she deserve?' I say.

'Ailish, don't be so cheeky.' Mammy says.

A children-should-be-seen and not heard glare. But. My

heart is racing and my shoulders feel tight and I want to know. Did she deserve something else, some other kind of punishment, but not that? Not what? Not cancer? Not death?

I move aimlessly, room to room. Try to go upstairs, hide in a bedroom, but Sarah and her friends are sitting on the return, their voices pitched high and giggly. It's freezing outside, Joe and his pals are talking loudly. Laughing. I wander past the scullery. Hear whispering. The door is ajar. Daddy and Auntie Elena are standing, heads bent into each other, his hand resting, fingers splayed, on the small of her back. Whispering and laughing. I don't hear what they are saying, but my head is filled with a terrible buzzing, as if a fire alarm has gone off. I turn sharp on the heel of my shoe, flee back to Mammy and the neighbour.

'Terrible, poor Carmel. Terrible,' the woman says.

'How did the Mass go?'

'It was fine.'

'Did you have many?'

'About thirty, I think. Family. Some of her neighbours.'

You squirm in the chair. Uncross your arms. Recross them.

'How …'

'How do I feel? I feel fine. It was fine. I am fine. Everything is fine.'

'Fine?'

'Fine.'

'Okay.'

You look to the window. The day outside is sunny.

'It was hard,' you say.

'How?'

'Raw. Elena was very upset.'

'About your mother?'

'No. I mean, yes, but more about Brendan. Upset looking

at Frank. The state of him now. I don't know. It was hard. Her generation is disintegrating around her.'

'Her children were there?'

'Yes. Not all of them, Louise and Ronan, Sarah and Michael. Their kids. Not Joe.'

'Michael was there?'

You hesitate.

'Yes. Michael is always there.'

4

August 1985

I wander the streets of Portobello looking for an address that matches my mother's cursive script on champagne-coloured Basildon Bond.

It's late August and Barbara has taken off to Medjugorje, a pilgrimage with some of her friends from the doctor's surgery, inspired, maybe, by the infestation of moving statues which has gripped the country all summer. Her devotion to the Virgin has grown new fervour since Frank moved to Galway during the week. Early morning Masses, the rosary beads never far from her fingers. A promotion, she says. My father is setting up a new department, EEC agricultural grants, don't you know. He's not coming home this weekend, he often doesn't, for reasons unspecified, Fiona and her mother are in Paris, and I'm not old enough to be trusted home alone.

So. Here I am. Traipsing rows of red-bricked houses, searching for one that might contain my cousins. Sarah, second-year psychology student in UCD. Louisa, first-year trainee nurse in the Adelaide Hospital. I'm wearing my current best outfit – light brown dungarees, stripy shirt, new low-heeled tan court shoes. A bid for style over practicality. I can feel a blister ready to pop on the little toe of my right foot, another bubbling on my left ankle.

I haven't seen much of my cousins since Granny died. Barbara isn't keen to visit Tullamore anymore. She went back to work the day after the funeral, against all advice, arguing we needed the money. Granny had left her a few thousand in the will. The farm went to Brendan, as expected. But. She's not happy. A pervasive discontent creeps out in sly remarks:

'Well for him, he can afford to send Elena and the children to Spain for six weeks,' she might say.

Not to be outdone, and to make a point of it, she invested some of her inheritance taking us all to Italy for a fortnight last summer. A visit to Rome, to see the Pope. July heat belting down on us at 10am in St Peter's Square, early to avoid queues that never materialised in the thirty-plus-degree day. Sodden ciabatta-and-parmesan-and-tomato sandwiches in the small white plastic bags she'd brought with her from home. It had been a big deal for Barbara, seeing the Pope, the whole trip. An event to drop over the wall in conversation with Kathleen Dunne. Her first time in an aeroplane. Mine too. She hailed it as an unheard-of-treat but, while I was happy to be saying I was going *somewhere,* many of my school friends go on holidays several times a year and the demand for gratitude put me in pissy form, all teenage pimply angst, gawk and sunburnt displacement. Complaints in queues and suspicious food pushed around plates in expensive trattoria.

She tells me I ruined the experience.

Which might be why I'm here now, knocking on a blue door, the low heat of a Friday late-afternoon snaking around my ankles. Windows like eyes, watching, judging my duffel bag, my school satchel, full of books though term hasn't started yet. When Louisa eventually answers, I'm rehearsing carefully constructed sentences, trying them out on my lips, a plan to head back home, say they weren't there, must have forgotten, gone home themselves ...

'Hi,' I say.

Smile.

Louisa is eighteen now, her early promise of beauty unfulfilled, sunk in two stone too many for her small frame, an unflattering white grandfather shirt, straining jeans.

'Oh ... Ailish, yeah ... Mama said you were coming.'

There's a distinct hesitation before my name, as if I am some randomer, one of many cousins, maybe, who used to infiltrate her childhood home. A pause which suggests she is struggling to place me in the context of her day. I stand. Wait for her to move aside, welcome me in. Some instruction. Clear my throat, shuffle the bags, banging at my shins.

'Oh,' she says. 'Are you coming in?'

I follow her through a claustrophobic anteroom, coats puffed on a wall rack, a grubby fuse box, black markings, stark in the daylight thrown by the open door, on into a largish sitting room. Either side of the fireplace is lined with white-painted MDF shelves, a few books, a small pile of records, a couple of small Lladró ornaments. A print of *The Kiss* by Klimt adorns the opposite wall, complementing an aged and naked terracotta-coloured sofa. There's an air of half-effort, as if somebody made a good start on the decor, then couldn't be bothered to finish the job, a bleakness somehow underscored by a lonely earthenware pot carrying the remains of long-dead red roses, squat on the dining table.

Barbara-in-my-head says: *You'd think two girls would take care of the place, seeing as their father paid a fortune for it.*

Brendan bought this house as an investment, he said, to save on rent for the cousins during their college years in Dublin. And the thought of her little brother with notions of himself as a man of property is too much now for my mother.

'I think Elena had an inheritance too,' Frank said. Once. To my mother's lips, disappeared in a thin line.

The room smells of smoke and patchouli. The variegated cream tiles on the fireplace are chipped, the exposed grouting grubby, a corner coloured lead with pencil. I place my bags beside the sofa, and we stand. I look around, vaguely, and so does Louisa. Wary assessing glances. I shift on sore feet, waiting to be asked to sit, to be shown, maybe, to a bedroom. Expectation dwindling. We search for something to say, struggle to find something in common. I consider proffering information about school, try to come up with something relevant. But. I'm unsure of the rules. Afraid to open myself up to, what – judgement? Ridicule? We're grown now, young women. We should be past this. I should be past this. Past my assumption the cousins think because I live in Dublin and go to a private school, I have notions about myself. I don't. Or, perhaps, I do, but I don't want them to think I do.

I break first:

'Do you like the nursing?'

'It's all right.'

A whiff of something fried long ago, maybe from the kitchen.

'Like, you're a bit of a skivvy for them. At first. But I'm sure it'll get better. Or I'll transfer to another hospital. Or something.'

I nod. Play with the pocket of my dungarees. Furl a fingertip around a stud.

'Would you like a cup of tea?'

Relief.

'Yes, thanks, I'd love one. Is Sarah here?'

'She's upstairs. In the shower. Getting ready.'

'Is she going out?'

'Yeah ... we're heading into town, probably the Baggot Inn. Later. Joe's coming up on the train.'

I thought I'd be sitting awkward with the girls watching *The Late Late Show*, or in a bedroom, on my own, studying. I hadn't factored in being home alone in a strange house. Or worse: socialising with them. Or, also: Joe.

* * *

'Michael is sleeping on the sofa,' Sarah says. 'It pulls out into a bed.'

Unaware of the effect these words have when they land in the soft part of my brain that daydreams about boys. I don't have much experience yet, but any boys I have met are secretly measured against Michael. That moment in the kitchen four years ago. His kindness. His eyes. His lips. Stupid, really.

There are two bedrooms. When they moved in Louisa won the double bed on the flip of a ten-pence piece, they tell me, so Sarah is in the one with twin beds. It is debated the best place for me is topping and tailing in this room, the spare bed, with Louisa, as Joe is bringing his girlfriend, Helen, over. Has paid Louisa a tenner to vacate her room for the night. She doesn't mind, she needs the money, she says. Anyway, she hints with mischief, Sarah may not need her bed either. The words sending a cold claw into my chest, stifling my breath. Are Sarah and Michael ...? Well, it's logical.

Sarah is a goddess. She sits now, regarding me, finely turned fingers caressing the filter of a cigarette, hand extended elegantly from a kimono-style dressing gown. A pattern of bougainvillea on navy silk. Her hair is wet, she has not a scrap of make-up on. I am mesmerised.

'You can't go out in that,' she says.

A small frown playing between her eyebrows.

'I'm sure I have something you can borrow. What size are you? A ten?'

I nod dumbly. The handful of non-school clothes I own are a ten or a twelve. I think. All pretence of teenage sophistication flees my body like a swarm of disturbed bees. I am a child again. A doll for my cousins to dress.

'Are the glasses essential?' Louisa says.

Her head to one side, palms square around a mug adorned with a fast-fading engagement photo of Charles and Diana.

'Only if I want to see,' I say.

They laugh. It feels good.

'Well, if we're heading to the Maggot Bin, good eyesight definitely isn't a plus,' Sarah says.

'I can do her make-up,' Louisa says.

'I have a dress that might work.'

'The blue one?'

'Yep.'

'I was just thinking that would be perfect. Bring out her eyes. Red belt?'

'Maybe. What size shoe do you take?'

'Four.'

'*Hmmm*,' Sarah says. 'We're both sixes.'

They look at my shoes – my pride – in critical unison.

'Bit frumpy with the blue dress,' Louisa says.

'They might look okay with my black skirt, a T-shirt?'

'Do we have time to wash her hair?'

I sip my tea, exchange my body as currency for acceptance. Find it a small price.

* * *

My reflection stares back from a mirror askew on a kitchen table strewn with smeared and dusty Constance Carroll, Rimmel, No. 7. Cotton wool, tissues, cheap brushes. The room is tight with other random paraphernalia, a sole window catching the swansong light of evening. Even without my glasses I can see Louisa has a heavy hand, wonder if it is politic to subdue the garish blues and reds, look with envy as Sarah applies her own mascara with restraint. Understand why 'less is more'.

'You look lovely,' Louisa says.

'Jesus, Lou, what have you done to her? We can't have her going out like that.'

'What's wrong with you, she looks perfect.'

All of us laughing now.

* * *

Sarah is removing excess product with a cotton-wool ball when the boys arrive. My eyes are thick with Simple cleanser, a fine film web across my eyelashes. A creamy sting. They've brought fish and chips, the sharp sweet smell of malt vinegar. Joe throws me a grumpy sort of nod, Michael smiles shyly. They are twenty now, Joe broad like Uncle Brendan, Michael, a head higher, the type of tall that feels the need to stoop. My face ignites.

'Ailish is staying for the weekend,' Sarah says.

Joe grunts. A noise that's neither approval nor disapproval.

I try to render myself invisible, self-consciously pull at the dressing gown Louisa lent me, pink and fluffy, like something Barbara would wear, a world away from the sophistication of Sarah's, which has slipped to reveal inches more thigh, right leg folded over left, her calf taut in a way that makes me think she'll end up with cramp.

'All good?' she says to Michael. Casually. Not casually.

'All right, yeah,' he says.

'The train was packed,' Joe says.

'They're all up for the match on Sunday,' Michael says.

He sits awkward on the arm of the sofa. I try to avoid his

eye, imagine he is trying to avoid mine. We are successful. Or maybe only I am successful.

'Did you get tickets?' Louisa says.

'I did, but only three,' Joe says

'Ah, feck ye, anyway. We'll have to draw straws.'

'Youngest stays behind, dems the rules.'

'You bollix, that's not going to work anymore. My days of being left behind are over.'

'Did you decide where we're going tonight?' Sarah says.

'A few of the lads are meeting in Toners, then probably the Baggot. If we can get Inn. *Boom boom*,' Joe says.

Nobody laughs.

We eat the fish and chips. The boys have brought cans of Harp, Sarah fetches Black Tower from the fridge, pours it into cups.

'Have some,' Louisa says.

'I'm grand,' I say.

'It's lovely,' Sarah says. 'Go on.'

Reluctantly, I sip on a cupful. Joe looks at me over the top of his can.

'How old are you?'

Accusatory. Assessing. No acknowledgement of shared history, no attempt to do the maths.

'Sixteen.'

He looks at Sarah, twitches an eyebrow.

'She won't get into the Baggot. She won't even get into Toners.'

'We'll redo the make-up, dress her up, it'll be grand,' Louisa says.

'I can stay here,' I say.

But I'm already warm from wine and want, desire to be part of the gang. To be in Michael's company. If only to observe him. Compare him with the version grown in my imaginings.

'When we're done with you, nobody will even think of asking for ID,' Sarah says.

They decide on a black dress with a ra-ra skirt. It makes me look sophisticated, they say. Older. Looks okay with the shoes. Sarah works my hair with a crimper, reapplies make-up, judiciously.

'You really do have lovely eyes,' she says.

She smells of Anaïs Anaïs. Luxuriant brown curls and skin so perfect, creamy and glowing, she might have stepped out of an advertisement. I stifle an urge to touch her. She bites on her lower lip as she works. She's wearing a white cheesecloth gypsy-style outfit with natural ease, at odds with Louisa's stripy T-shirt dress, horizontal lines which do nothing for her figure.

*　*　*

We're a motley crew, falling down the evening colours of the canal. The wine hitting my head now, white tips of locks looming ominous, my mother's voice in my head: *Keep clear of the canal, don't walk too close.*

As if I might jump in, be attacked by a random swan.

Joe's girlfriend, Helen, meets us en route. A vague 'Hi', her eyes only for Joe. They pull ahead, leaving Michael and Sarah in the middle, Louisa and I bringing up the rear.

'They make a good-looking couple, don't they?' she says.

And my stomach lurches.

'Joe and Helen? I say.

'Michael and Sarah.'

'Are they going together?'

Words which come out scratchy. Would betray me, if Louisa was attuned to hear.

'Well, no, not exactly. They've got off with each other, like a couple of times, but he hasn't asked her to go with him. Yet. Maybe tonight.'

'But she likes him?'

'She does, yeah. Who wouldn't? Sure isn't he a ride?'

*　*　*

The pub is packed, bodies squished like savage sardines, drinks flying dangerously, and, from my average five-foot five perspective, a surfeit of body odour. Joe, who is working on the farm, and therefore flush, offers to get a round. I only have a fiver in my purse, which won't be enough to reciprocate. And I don't know much about pub life, but I know this is expected. I order a Coca-Cola. A part of me panicking, wondering if I can head back to the house. Borrow money off Louisa. But how to pay it back?

'You look lovely,' Michael says.

Looming from the crowd, vacuuming the air with a look I don't know how to read. His eyes steady on mine.

'Oh, I ... I look ridiculous.'

Blush.

He is still. A composed silence. As if he is scanning my brain, reading my secrets.

'No. You look lovely.'

Sarah appears at his side, all hoops and white-tooth smiles, her tinkly laugh fighting background noise and she reaches up and says something into his ear and he laughs too. They are gone in a blur of shoulders and elbows and jostling colour, and I am talking to Louisa, who is slurring.

'Most of them just want to marry a doctor,' she says. 'Maybe I do too, you know? I don't know yet. But maybe. If this Cambridge diet works. I'm starting it on Monday, did I tell you?'

'You did.'

'Fuck it. Like *fuck it*. I know I need to lose a bit, you know? I do, don't I?'

'You look perfect.'

'Well, you're a skinny bitch, you would say that, wouldn't you? Bet you've never had a fat day in your life. Shakes. That's all they give you, you know? Shakes. One for breakfast, one for lunch, and then your dinner. Shit. Fuck. Don't know if I can do it.'

'I'm sure you can, if you put your mind to it.'

'I will. It's hard, you know, Ailish? Having a sister like Sarah. People compare.'

And I can't, in honesty, deny this.

Joe is talking with a group of friends, Helen standing on the periphery. I catch her eye, and we smile. Louisa and I shift in her direction, form a female group on the edge of the lads.

'So you're Aileen?' she says.

'Ailish.'

'Oh. Yeah. Joe said.'

'What did he say?'

'Just you're his cousin.'

Along with the foreignness of the hues and the noise and smells, a beetle of paranoia invades my brain. Starts to burrow. I wonder how my cousins portray me when they talk to their friends. I try to quell that awkward child still alive in me, still craving acceptance into a club in which she is only eligible for associate membership. At best. We're practically adults and this is a random encounter. We probably won't see each other again for years. I have my own full and busy life. School is starting again. Exams and debating and hockey and friends and boys and parties. All the rituals of autumn. Barbara's random trials and ministrations. Frank. Frank, who might show up at any time or not at all. Who might be here, there or anywhere. Might be in Galway, as he said. Might be over there now at the bar, chatting up a barmaid. Might be in Tullamore with Elena, right at this moment, for all I know. For all Barbara knows. Or Brendan. And do these guys know? Is Frank a regular caller at the house when their father is away at tractor fairs or whatever farmers do? Do they suspect what I do? Worse, do they know? And are they whispering about it when I'm not around?

'C'mon, we're heading now,' Joe says.

We finish our drinks dutifully and follow him.

* * *

A heaving mess of fabric and flesh, smoke from cigarettes and something I will later identify as weed, we queue outside the Baggot Inn. Inky lit pavements pockmarked with chewing gum, slimy trails of piss and vomit. Violently chipped doorways. Michael and Sarah are entwined, a vibe between them, heads inclined. Joe is at the door negotiating with a man who looks like an oversized toddler, a tattoo of a creeping snake curling around his left ear. I'm worried about Louisa, who has disappeared.

'She met some nurse friends,' Helen says.

I'm sober now, disconnected, lost. Even though they are standing beside me, they have continued a journey without me. I've no map to help me catch up. Sarah wobbles, trips, knocks into Michael. Giggles. He rights her and stands back, something in his movement unimpressed. A small stiffening of his shoulder. Subtle. Telling. I think: she's messing all this up. And I'm upset with her and angry with her and something else I can't name. She sways. I put a hand out to steady her. Her elegant ringed fingers grasp at a groove in a door frame. She lurches. She spews.

'Oh, for fuck's sake,' Michael says.

Her body wracks and spasms. I put my arm around her. Try to contain her away from the crowd. When she finishes, she looks up, her lipstick smudged, mascara streaks cracking her cheeks.

'We have to get her home,' I say.

Michael looks to Joe, who is motioning Helen inside now, denim jacket astride her shoulders, ponytail oscillating, the low thrum of the beat inside vibrating the ground, pulling her like a Pied Piper. Pulling all of us.

Sarah hurls again, falls forward. Shakes violently. A look passes between the boys. A resigned understanding.

'I'll take her home,' Michael says. 'You go on.'

I look around and realise that if he does, Louisa is missing in action and Helen is with Joe. I'm on my own. I panic.

'I'll help,' I say.

'No taxi will take us,'

One whizzes by.

'We can walk her,' I say.

'It'll take forever.'

'We don't have an option, do we? If you help me get her home I can mind her from there. You'll be back here within an hour, if you're that keen.'

'That's not what I meant. Sorry. Of course we have to get her home. It's just a pain. Your night is ruined too.'

I say nothing. I'm cross with this big galoot for some unfathomable reason. Maybe a fathomable reason. We pick our way back to Portobello, an awkward orchestration of limbs and torsos.

We push-pull Sarah upstairs and onto the bed. The stench off her is pungent, overpowering in the small room. I open the window. Shoo Michael, remove her soiled skirt and top. It's too difficult to manoeuvre the duvet to cover her, so I find a small blanket and arrange that around her instead. Tuck down the sides. Barbara used to do this sometimes, I think. A half-memory. Ephemeral. Unexpected tenderness. A missing of something.

I see myself, a shadow form, in the ill-lit wall mirror. Almost as much of a mess as Sarah. I take off the dress, my night of sophistication now mingled with hers on nylon carpet. I'm bone tired and I need to remove the make-up, but the cleanser and moisturiser are in the bathroom downstairs. For some reason I still cannot own, will never own, I stand, a half-formed half-woman, in the exotic confines of a student bedroom only a few miles but a lifetime away from home, and I don't take my brushed cotton pyjamas from my bag. I don't take the fluffy pink dressing gown Barbara would be delighted with off the end of the other single bed. I take Sarah's dressing gown, from the end of Sarah's bed, the garment I so coveted earlier, and I slip my small frame into its silky folds. A knowing in me, yet not in me, as if I am compelled by some external force to emulate her, to steal her skin.

The stairs are uncarpeted, my bare heel slips on the third step and I land on my arse in the sitting room. Hard. Loud.

'*Fuck!*

'Jesus Christ, are you all right?'

I'd thought he was gone. I'm not all right. My left elbow screams pain.

'I'm fine.'

I stand quickly, proud, pull the dressing gown closed, double-knot the belt.

'You're not fine,' he says. 'That was a massive thump.'

My eyes sting. I clutch my elbow.

'I gave it a bit of a bang. That's all.'

'Let's see.'

I lift the sleeve of the gown and we examine my elbow together. His head bent towards mine, teen longing and hours spent looking at Nick Heyward posters and comparing their lips, the cleft in their chins, the slight overbite, converge in a moment. I belch. Loudly. It sits, impolite, on the air between us. I blush. He laughs. I laugh, and the embarrassment is transformed into a delicious, shared thing.

'Sorry,' I say.

'You're in shock. Ice, or peas. They must have something in the fridge.'

'I'm grand, you're heading back into town.'

'Not in this, I'm not.' He indicates his Offaly jersey. 'Sure I'd be only mauled by the women.'

I laugh.

'It must be ruined. Your shirt.'

'Your dress.'

'Sarah's dress.'

'It looked better on you.'

And then:

'Sorry,' he says.

Every part of me tingles. I wonder if this is what it is like to have an out-of-body experience. I sit on the sofa, pull the dressing gown tight, and he goes to the kitchen, the fridge. My brain in overdrive trying to figure this new landscape.

'Do you want a beer? There's no wine left.'

And I could say: 'No, thanks, but if there's a Coke, I'd love one.' Or I could say: 'D'you know, I'd murder a cup of tea.'

But what I do say is: 'Beer would be grand. Thanks'.

He brings back two cans and a packet of peas covered in a tea towel. He click-pulls the ring on one of the cans and hands it to me, lifts the sleeve of the dressing gown, fixes the peas in place. Sits beside me. Pulls the ring on the other can. Sips.

'It'll stop it swelling,' he says. 'It's what we do when we get a hurling injury.'

I know so little about him, bar a vague notion he works on the farm with his dad, like Joe. For all my tentative research, covert quizzing of my mother over the years, I have impressions, not detail.

'Do you play?'

'I did, when I was at home. I'm up in UCD now, Ag Science.'

'Oh.'

A 40-watt bulb filters meekly through the tasselled shade of the standard lamp. A yellow light. A mellow light

'Do you like it?' I say. 'UCD?'

'Yeah, it's all right. It'll be useful like. When I'm back working on the farm. How about you?'

I hesitate. All hormonal churn. I don't want to say 'I'm doing my Leaving Cert next year', own my schoolgirl credentials, not here, not now, with the silk of Sarah's dressing gown sitting light on skin quivery with proximity.

'I want to do Law,' I say.

And I do. For all I might play it down with my cousins, I have dreams and ambitions and I have big notions. Encouraged by my parents. Supported by my teachers.

'UCD?'

'Probably.'

'Cool.'

We swig on the cans.

'Will I put on some music?' he says.

'Sure.'

He goes to the record player, searches the haphazard selection of vinyl beside it.

'It'll all be CDs before we know it.'

'D'you think Sarah will be okay?'

'She went out like a light. That'll be it until the morning.'

'We should probably keep an eye on her, in case she vomits again.'

'Probably.'

'I didn't think she'd drunk so much.'

'She was smoking and had a hip flask on the go. You know what she's like.'

But I don't. I watch him sideways, the groove of his upper lip. I have kissed two boys before now: one, to the strains of Ultravox's *Vienna*, a random fella at an Old Wesley disco; two, the brother of a friend, a frantic half-fumble in a utility room at a severely supervised party. Neither experience was formative. I realise I am staring.

'Desperate selection,' he says. 'Fun Boy Three? Paul Young, *huh*. How about Dire Straits?'

'Sure.'

He puts it on the deck, flicks a lever and the arm moves slowly while he makes his way back to the couch. Sits down again, carefully, lightly.

Closer now.

'Do you still miss your granny?'

I reach deep to find and form words. Fail.

'Like, I felt for you, y'know, when I met you at the funeral that time.'

Shiver.

Thrill.

Seen. Recognised in a moment. Remembered.

'Like, I remember her well from when I was little playing with Joe. Always had some kind of biscuit or cake for us. She was a great woman.'

'She was.'

A tear grows. And I'm not sure if it's for Granny or if it's the beer or if it's overwhelm at the strangeness of the situation. How am I here, in this place, now, with Michael? It seems impossible.

'Sorry. I didn't mean to upset you.'

He puts a thumb out to wipe the tear away. Traces it across my cheek. A touch perfectly timed with the opening riff of the song: *Romeo and Juliet.*

'Ah here,' he says.

His arm snaking around my shoulder, pulling me into him. Kissing the top of my head.

'I'm an awful gobshite.'

''S okay.'

'I didn't mean to upset you. '

I'm enveloped in his scent. Musk and beer and fabric softener. Underneath the dressing gown, underneath my broderie anglaise bra, my overwashed knicker-elastic, my body is responding to a rush of hormones. Taut. Brittle. Frangible. I pull back, inadvertently create enough space to enable an essential moment of eye contact.

Pause.

Shiver.

His palm, padded, calloused, cups the side of my face, fingers push through hair, to the back of my neck. He pulls me forward. His lips. Those lips. On mine.

Thrill.

Shiver.

Long moments. Exploring. Tongues. Teeth. That overbite. Moving now, arms over shoulders and under armpits, tiny beside him, hands, hands everywhere, hands pulling me onto his lap, astride, the dressing gown, knot undone, fumble, gone, fumble, the bra, gone, stubble brushing nipple, lips and hips and hands employed on waist, breasts, *shiver, thrill,* lower, *shiver;* Fiona and I, in the garden, eating ice cream, reading Anaïs Nin, aloud; Frank's badly hidden porn, girls with blue eyeshadow, differing body shapes and shades, *shiver, thrill;* muted noises, Frank, Barbara, hands over ears, *shiver;* panties gone, limbs, liquid, Michael, tender, touching, *shiver, thrill;* Barbara-in-my-head, men will say anything for this, *shiver;* Michael-here-and-now, his voice, dark, thick, gelatinous:

'Are you okay? I can stop ...'

Pause.

Shiver.

Thrill.

'Don't. Don't stop.'

5

Mid-morning light spills through slits in cheap curtains. Faded mauve carnations sprawled on dirty white cotton, inadequate to repel the day. I'm at the head of the bed by virtue of the fact I got into it first. Louisa lies solid down the other end, so entirely unresponsive I'm amazed – and relieved – she made it home. The bed opposite is empty. Sarah missing. I'm wearing my brushed cotton pyjamas. My head is thick, teeth woolly. Everything blurred.

'I always thought you were lovely,' he'd said. 'I'd see you in Mass, standing with your family. You looked ... I don't know, just different? Like you were taking all of it in and coming to your own conclusions? Jesus, that sounds fecking stupid, sorry. I just mean, I noticed you.'

'I never noticed you noticing me.'

My memories of Mass in Tullamore are fraught, a parade on a public tightrope, a show. A potential to fail, to fall oblivious into some trap of public misbehaviour which might be lurking in the aisles like quicksand. It left little space for observation.

That somebody – this boy – might have been watching. That he might have thought I was lovely. Implausible.

* * *

We lay entwined in the remnants of our clothing. A scuffle at the door alerted us. Scrabbling bodies, poorly controlled, intoxicated, battling with keys. I panicked, jumped, grabbed the robe, my underwear, fled upstairs, aware, unaware, of my nakedness. Into my pyjamas, under the duvet, eyes sticky with mascara, before I heard them fall through the door.

'Give us a hand,' Joe yelled.

Muffled sounds of angst and swearing. Louisa was in a state. The boys manhandled her dead weight awkwardly up the stairs and onto the end of the bed I was lying in. As they pulled and shoved, I stirred, pretended to be asleep, pretended to wake only a little, tried to communicate telepathically with Michael through the gloom. I could make out the shape of him, but his features were darkened, unreadable. Shifting Louisa's bulk in whispers to accommodate her feet and legs and bum with mine. I lay there desperate for a sign, a secret word, a cough, a touch. Anything that might legitimise what had happened, relieve the heavy mantle of guilt which was starting to settle into the molecules of me.

* * *

Now the guilt has solidified. Taken over, heavy in my head and heart and limbs. I am paralysed. Acutely aware of clunking kitchen sounds as somebody attempts to prepare food. Low voices, cracked laughter, somebody responding to a joke or a bitchy comment.

Are they laughing at me?

A raging shame engulfs me. Inhabits me. I imagine Michael sitting there, regaling them with the story of how I fell down the stairs in Sarah's dressing gown, how he'd mistakenly thought I was her, but really I'm only a townie slut, and he had a good time ... But. But. He would never say this. He thought I was lovely. He thinks I am lovely. And he surely thinks Sarah is lovely too, how could he not, hasn't he known her all his life, wasn't he, only earlier last night, keen to be in a relationship with her, which, given how close their families are, would, could, only be serious? Jesus. What have I done?

What have I done?

At the foot of the bed, Louisa snores, a sharp, frilly sound that rises to a crescendo. And stops. And starts. And stops. A whirring towards wakefulness. The air stale with sweat and alcohol. Cigarette smoke.

Sarah appears in the doorway. She's up and dressed, white T-shirt and blue jeans, face clean, hair scrapped back in a ponytail. A vision of purity. Innocence.

'Are you coming down for breakfast?' she says. 'I've made a fry-up. Is she alive?'

Motions towards Louisa, who farts loudly.

'Guess that answers that. C'mon, the lads will eat the lot if you don't move fast.'

I move obediently as a sleepwalker. A wraith navigating a

nightmare. Sarah picks up an ornate silvered hand mirror from her locker, checks the sculpted contours of her face carefully, wipes a stray fleck of matter from her eye. Fires the mirror on her bed.

'Jesus, I feel rough. Come down in your pyjamas, nobody will care.'

I pick up the clothes I planned to wear today. Clean underwear. Move to the bathroom. Take my pyjamas off. The crotch is stained with blood. I feel sick. Wash myself. Pour new me into yesterday's dungarees. A fresh T-shirt. Run a brush through my hair. Eyes smudged new with experience stare back at me. I think: last night is a landmark, a milestone, a line – something I will remember now forever. Regardless. A sick knowledge. Settling. This: virginity lost. Always tainted. My cousin's friend. My cousin's boyfriend. Tendrils of relationships, growing, gnarling, snarling beanstalks. Choking. Everything. Bile hits the back of my throat, slides into my mouth. Jesus. Jesus. Barbara would kill me if she knew. Will kill me. If she finds out. March me to Father Cleary for confession, a million Hail Marys, life forever now on my knees. Repenting. This despicable act. Sister John, orating about sins of the flesh. Sister Bríd's high hot cheeks, lips wet with vindication.

'I knew you'd let us down, Ailish McCarthy. No better than you should be, for all your high marks, all your *potential*. All your hanging about with Fiona Fitzpatrick. Your grandiose notions. You're a slut. Just like the rest of them.'

Slut.

But.

Slut.

I'm careful on the stairs. Wobble on the third step. Shoe sides reacquainted with blisters they burst yesterday. Pay my penance with pain. Offer it up for leniency.

'Well. at least there's one woman in the family who didn't disgrace herself last night,' Joe says.

He's sitting with Helen on the sofa, eating off plates on their laps, large mugs of tea on a low table. The smell. So ordinary. The room. In daylight. I try to smile, frozen, the bubbled glass of the half-door to the hall a beacon calling me, screaming: *RUN.*

'Morning,' Michael says.

Standing in the doorway to the kitchen. He smiles. A lopsided beauty. But at the room. Won't catch my eye. My stomach jumps. Freefalls.

'Morning,' I say.

'Did you sleep okay?' Helen says.

'How could she, with Louisa like a lump of lard at the end of the bed?' Sarah says.

She's standing behind Michael, tickling the sides of his waist to move him along into the room, her hand resting comfortably on his hip. A gesture so intimate I almost vomit.

'You can't talk,' Joe says.

'Judge Joe, like you're a saint yourself,' Sarah says.

'He just never gets caught,' Helen says.

And they laugh, easy in each other's company, the way people who have known each other all their lives sometimes are.

Beyond the sashed window, the houses glisten clean as red-brick ghosts, all imperfections erased in searing sunlight. The promise of breath calling me: *RUN*.

'I'm sorry you didn't get to go to the gig,' Sarah says. 'I hadn't eaten all day, didn't realise how it would hit me. Michael said you were a great help bringing me home.'

She hands me a plate of fried food, an egg congealing in a gritty grease.

'Sit down here,' Helen says, vacating the spot beside Joe. 'I'm going for a shower.'

Michael, still standing, still avoiding my eye, nods a g'wan, and I'm grateful for even this acknowledgement.

I sit down. I don't know what else to do. I can't speak. Am afraid to. Afraid that if I even open my mouth it might say, might shriek: *Michael and I had sex here last night!* On this sofa. A kiss underneath *The Kiss*. More than a kiss. What do you think of that? But I can't. Speak.

'I'm going down to the shop for bread,' Michael says.

'We have some,' Sarah says.

'You've no batch.'

'I don't think they do it in Dublin? Sure we've plenty of sliced pan. We can go later, I need to get something for dinner anyway.'

'I could do with the walk.'

'Well, wait up then, I'll check on Louisa and come with you.'

I sit in a trance, as if I am on stage, an actor in a play who has forgotten her lines. As he prepares to go, I try to catch Michael's eye again, and this time I do, but the look that comes back is unknowable. Ambiguous. Maybe conspiratorial. Maybe apologetic.

'See you in a bit,' he says, walking towards the door, Sarah following, grabbing a jacket from the rack.

And he is gone.

I'm alone, on the sofa, with Joe. His thighs thick in jeans frayed at the knee, his hand resting, fingers thrumming as if tapping out a code.

I think: he knows.

I think: *RUN.*

'Better wash these up,' I say, lifting my plate and cutlery. Hoarse.

Joe says nothing.

I leave the sudsy ware to dry on the draining board. Climb the stairs. Don't look at Joe.

Still sitting.

Still saying nothing.

Louisa is half-awake now. Groaning.

'Jesus, my head,' she says.

I pack my bag.

'Are you going?'

'Mammy's home,' I say. 'She has an emergency, she wants me back.'

'Is everything all right?'

'Yeah, fine. Just a Barbara thing.'

Unquestionable. A Barbara thing.

'Oh.'

I make my way downstairs. Joe is gone. The sofa empty. I slip the latch, slide out and close the door quietly. Start walking. Keep walking. The air is fresh with autumn, the willow leaves already rusting. Mid-morning swans ripple surface sunlight on the dark waters of the canal. I move at a steady pace. Over Leeson Street bridge, on through the Georgian splendour of Donnybrook, past the pub and the shops, past Bus Éireann, past RTÉ, past the Montrose Hotel, Stillorgan, all the way out the N11. Wanting to cry. Not wanting to cry. Not able to cry. Numb. By the time I reach home, my feet are in shreds.

'I've never told anybody,' you say. 'About Michael.'

Rain is lashing the small window. The room warm. Confessional.

'Not even the people who know the rest of it.'

'Why do you think that is?'

You start to play with your wedding ring. Realise this. Stop.

'Fear? The complication of it. Their opinions and dissection of it. They would find a way to make it their business. It's not their business.'

'Who are "they"?'

'They. Others. The pack. Those who sit in judgement.'

'Do they have faces?'

'Do they need them?'

'Well, it might help to be able to identify your enemy.'

'The *Daily Mail* brigade. That mentality. Sniffers of dirt. The neighbours.'

'Is this a big thing for you, what the neighbours think?'

'It was a big thing for my mother.'

'That's not what I asked.'

'It's not relevant in this case anyway.'

'How do you mean?'

'I mean, apart from here, now, I would never tell anybody about Michael. Regardless.'

'Why not?'

'It's still too private. Still too dangerous.'

'Dangerous to whom?'

Shiver.

'Me.'

6

My period arrives a week later, earlier than expected. Pink and pretty in new white cotton underwear. Relief. Absolution. An answer to prayer-filled nights, suffused with the eerie green glow of a lava lamp. Deals with The Almighty. Deals with The Devil.

I reform. Wrap my errant flesh in repentant blue gabardine, starched collar, woollen jumper, fraying at the cuffs. Pull hair back from scrubbed face with tortoiseshell combs, scratched deep across my scalp, plunged into place with purpose. A Mass-going vision. Write intelligent observations in tiny script in exemplary notebooks, answer questions enthusiastically, control my thoughts and actions as if by force. By force. Actually.

Fiona is suspicious.

'It's the Leaving Cert,' I say. 'You might be able to afford to take it lightly. I can't.'

Fiona is not taking it lightly. She wants to do Medicine. Capital M. Every parent's Holy Grail. Though of all our parents, Yvonne cares least. Apart from core classes, Honours English, Irish, Maths, we have different subjects now. She is doing

Biology, Chemistry and Physics. French. I do History, Geography, Art. German. Although there was consternation over this flimsy choice, an earnest discussion over a rigid family dinner about points and options and subjectivity. But. Objectively, I can draw. I have a talent for colour. My bedroom walls are littered with portraits of Frank and Barbara. Granny. Fiona. But the sketchbook under my mattress is reserved for fantasies of Michael: his hair, his hands, his lips. The frustrating and elusive curve of Sarah's cheekbones. Sombre moments of self-torture, as treacherous as scoring my skin with a blade. I look in the mirror, cup my hand around my own face, but the palette of it is different. The ruling genetics are different.

* * *

There's a school disco at Halloween. No boys allowed. The consequence of a scandalous foray into a gym storeroom at an earlier event, which has resulted in a Fifth Year going missing. *Hush shush.* Sister John stalking halls, her face reminiscent of an ET told he can never go home. To permit a celebration at all is a compromise, won against her better judgement, every concession a personal battle, every leeway tinged with blame. Shame.

Fiona and I sit now, fit now, within a wider group of six. Middle-class girls of more or less modest means, daughters of architects, accountants, amorphous insurance company executives. None come from a house as basic as mine or as opulent as Fiona's. We have in common, maybe, nerdish tendencies. Good girls. We don't speak the language of the cool gang, the girls who hang after bands, talk knowingly of drugs and drink, casual sex and – shock – contraception. Rubber Johnnies and The Pill. *Blush. Hush.* Decorate their blue-and-yellow hessian schoolbags with CND symbols, wear keffiyeh and DIY hemlines, defy the nuns to challenge them. Neither do we fit with the rich kids, who flit to holiday homes in Spain or France or America. Talk of first-class flights and yacht clubs and ski trips. Of Gucci, Versace and Armani, brand names we have no reference for. Watches and rings and sacred milestones marked with money. Instead, we take snooty bookish high ground: Austen and the Brontës, to indicate soul. Irving, Adams, Herbert, contemporary relevance. Orwell, Kafka, Proust, to pose. Binchy, for solidarity. We affect to like the impressionists, cite Monet, Manet, Cezanne, as if we spend time in Paris. Paint Degas-like ballerinas. Covet the colour of Kandinsky and Klimt. Listen to jazz and artists we consider have an edge – Tom Waits, Mary Coughlan, U2 – whilst never missing Thursday *Top of the Pops*. Subversive Madonnas, traipsing terrazzo tiles to the beat of 'Like a Virgin'.

We hang with boys who are like us. Brothers and their friends. Safe spaces. Common ground. Awkward teens trying to figure their way to manhood parroting Monty Python. Focused on following their fathers into the right universities, the right careers. A middle-class Spielberg-led, Disney-fed dream. Boys who respect girls. Respectable girls. Watch porn for educational purposes only. Good partners, good prospects, good fathers. When the time is right. After the wedding.

They want to come to the all-girls disco, these boys. Specifically, Deirdre's brother, Mark, a twinkling redhead with reputed brains and an eye for mischief. An eye for me. I know this. He skirts and hovers. A freckle-faced vulture stalking his prey with sparkle and wink and wit. A mix missing only the magic of a man-boy from Tullamore.

'Sure it's fancy dress. You could sneak us in,' he says.

'G'wan, it'd be a laugh,' says his friend, James.

Who has a yen for Fiona, who has a yen, actually, for Mark.

We pass a late afternoon into evening in Fiona's eclectic basement kitchen, red-and-white-chequered oilcloth laden with joke shop paraphernalia, wigs and make-up and prosthetics. Yvonne, floating on a cloud of kaftan, turns an amused blind eye to the sedition. Naggins of vodka, filing their way into glasses of orange juice. Clouding our judgement of what beauty might be.

A boy I will remember only as Moosey is a particular problem. The attributes that earned him his moniker are hard to hide. His hair is long and wavy, which helps, but the protuberant nose and ears are unconvincing as female, no matter how hilariously we try to prettify them. He is implausibly tall. The noise level rises.

We girls are a coven – six witches on the sexy side, Bangles wannabes, dresses made from black plastic bags, ragged in all the right places. Hair industriously backcombed, faces layered with make-up. Eyes like badgers.

By the time we trip up the steps to street level, there's a feeling the best of the party is over. By the time we walk the tree-lined avenue to the school, a whisper of sanity has set in. Barbara's reaction to my inevitable disgrace and expulsion: 'All the opportunities we gave you.' 'All you've cost us.' 'You've ruined your life.'

A buzz of fear fizzing through the vodka.

'This isn't going to work,' I say.

Margaret, prone to panic, looks at me smudgy-eyed, a sudden realisation, a spectre of her own mother floating on her shoulder. Deirdre is up ahead, all gung-ho. Fiona is wrapped in James, their skirts melding into one, ambling forward like lopsided Siamese twins. Mark is floating near me with patient intent. A rogue squad focused blearily on an uncertain target. It's Moosey who saves us.

'She's right, it's not worth it. Let's just go back to mine.'

We stop in the harsh glare of McDonald's for soakage. Mark tightens his co-ordinates and circles, but doesn't approach directly until we are on safe ground in Moosey's living room. On the sofa. I know the move is coming. It's awkward and immature. I'm a spiral and whirl of emotion. Mark is eminently suitable boyfriend material. Good family, polite, promising future. I like him. Barbara would approve. Frank would? Be relieved? Another tie severed.

But. He's not the man-boy from Tullamore. He's nothing like. I could remove this boy from my head without a backward glance. Nor is he a lover as depicted in *Cosmopolitan*. Suave, urbane. He would care about this: my virginity. Lack thereof. Would I have to, will I be able to, pretend? And while these thoughts ping from one neuron to another, his face is on mine, lips missing mine, a suffocation. His mouth moving rhythmically on my chin. I submit. I think: this is normal. The other is not. I am in control. I am not. His hand moves up the bin-liner, searching for the curve of my breast. Finds it. Squeezes it. Pain. Tenderness. Heaviness. If I'd noticed the change, I'd denied it. After all, I'd got my period. A week after the fact. Almost two months ago. But not since.

7

Barbara goes out on Tuesday nights. St. Vincent de Paul, co-ordinating the gathering and supply of second-hand goods for single mothers. Buggies, cots, sterilisers, and the like. Clothing. The group is run by Estelle Van Der Kamp O'Connor, a Dutch woman, married to an Irish businessman, living in a vast house on the Dalkey side of Killiney Hill. 'Too much money and too much time on her hands,' my father says. 'An over-egged sense of social responsibility.' he says. A heady mix my mother inhales. Estelle this, Estelle that. She drops her name into conversations randomly, identifies herself proudly as a satellite of this do-gooding-mothership, an unworthy acolyte.

They don't agree on everything, which causes Barbara visible dissonance. Estelle keeps her views contained for the most part – the greater good, respect for the charities she's involved in – but they were on opposite sides when it came to the Eighth Amendment debate. My mother is a staunch Catholic, committed to, if not overly vocal on, the equal rights of the unborn child to life, regardless of the woman's situation. Estelle is a declared feminist, championing, in her own elegant way, for women to have autonomy over their bodies, the right to control their fertility, a persistent rumour claiming she actively procures and distributes condoms to those in the know. In a confiding mother-daughter moment, Barbara shares with me a popular theory that Estelle might be on The Pill. After all she is in her late thirties, married a decade, and not a child to show for it. An effort not to ruin her figure is cited as a plausible reason.

Though her childbearing years are long gone now, I think the need for a baby has not gone off my mother. When we bump into a recipient of her charity's beneficence in a coffee shop with a ruddy-faced offspring, her face lights in a way I've never known. She balances the baby on her arm, bouncing and rocking it to quiet with a competence and ease alien to me. A halo of peace, the giving of comfort feeding her as much as the child. The sadness in her is pervasive – it reaches out and swallows me in its folds.

* * *

Tuesday nights I am usually home alone until about half past ten. I've only been able to get vodka. I'm assuming it will do the same trick as gin. My hand shaking, I turn the taps and run the bath. Test the temperature with my fingertips. I know it should be as hot as I can handle, but I don't know how I know this. The same way I knew the small changes to my body, the sore breasts, the darkened nipples, the heaviness in my pelvis, spelt trouble. Some savage instinct, information gathered by osmosis, whispered sisterly knowledge shared without structure. Maybe I read it in a book.

I half-fill the small glass. I'm wary about spirits, don't like the taste, and I'm conscious I need to stay in control. Conscious I'm going out of my mind, part of my brain detached, watching me from afar. Judging me. Ailish McCarthy. The Good Girl. Who would have thought it. I add orange juice. I sip. Balance the cocktail on the laundry basket beside the bath, take off my dressing gown, step in. *Uh uh uh.* Try not to slide. My feet and calves turn scarlet. I stand for a long time, firm on the non-slip bathmat, sip more alcohol. Lower myself in, grasp at the bath sides, find no purchase. Thighs and bottom immersed. *Breathe. Breathe.* Allow a small tear. Slither down. Cry some more. *Sip. Sip.* Consider the required ratio of hot liquid outside to hot liquid inside. *Sip.* Run more hot water. Watch as it pools around the burgeoning convex of my stomach. Mourn its flatness. *Sip.*

When I can stand it no more, I get out, dry myself, put on clean pyjamas, clean the bath, wash the glass, hide the vodka, go to bed. Get up, put a hopeful pad in my pants. Go back to bed. Hear the click as Barbara arrives home. Go to sleep. Eventually.

*　*　*

I go to school. An angsty zombie. When the bell rings I go straight to the toilets, check my pad. *Nothing. Every. Class. Wednesday over. Thursday over. Friday. Over.*

Ten weeks now, since The Event.

In Fiona's house, after school, I sneak a peek at her biology book. Reproduction. A fully formed foetus stares back at me. Tiny fingers and tiny toes. An alien head. Images from the referendum, which I largely ignored at the time, haunt me.

Ann Lovett.

Joanne Hayes.

Andrea Flynn, from down the road, growing round in a mist of whispers, fading from her daily path to some ghost universe, so quietly it seemed almost normal. This is something, the Universe tells me, my mother tells me, that happens only to stupid girls. Half-wits. Goms. Not all-Honours students from good homes like Ailish McCarthy. I have dreams and hopes and aspirations. My parents have expectations.

This. Cannot. Happen. To. Me.

* * *

I acquire the gin. I run the bath without using the cold tap. Add a kettle of boiling water. Pour a full glass and gulp it down neat in punishing mouthfuls.

Take that.

And that.

I. Will. Get. This. Thing. Out. Of. Me.

When the buzz starts to hit, after it has well set in, I brave myself for the water. Scalding now. I'm only vaguely aware of sizzling epidermis, the puckering, the pulling, the rush of fluid to blisters. I sit. *Splat.* Buttocks displacing the water soundly. A river between my reddening thighs. I immerse my stomach, swishing side to side, a pincer attack.

Not me. Not. Me.

I won't be forever tied to a stupid mistake with a stupid boy who hasn't even had the decency to contact me. Is probably off doing the same thing now with Sarah. Louisa. *Elena.*

My face crumples and I squeeze my eyelids tight, as if this might cauterise reality. Might vanquish the misery of existence. The pointless confusion and sadness which stalks, walks with us all, daily. Which has descended now, is concentrated here in this room, this cauldron of snot and tears and dirty bathwater.

I hear a click.

Freeze. Listen. Panic.

I try to jump up, but I stumble and thump down again. One leg over the side of the bath, fingers finding a groove, losing it, torso falling. Hits the laundry basket. Sends the glass flying against the sink. I watch as it splinters and sparkles into a zillion tiny pieces. Slow motion. Powdery diamonds coating the floor. I feel them underfoot. I don't feel them. They bring no familiar sting. Wasps, armed to do damage again. *Slip. Slide.* Red. Spilling. Pooling. From my foot. From my leg. On the floor.

Wet. Cold. Naked.

Perverse.

'Ailish, what on earth …?'

Barbara. Me.

An exchange which requires no words.

8

'We need to be sure,' Barbara says, statue-still in the bathroom.

I squat, pee in a cleaned-out jam jar, dressing gown askew, dignity dead.

I've only a hazy sense of the night before: screeching, pulling, getting up, falling down again. Tears. Recriminations. My mother's face etched hard with damnation. No words. The quiet worse.

She brings the sample to work in the clinic. Does whatever she has to do there. Arrives home. Sits stiff at the kitchen table, hands folded.

Eyes inward.

Confirms the diagnosis.

No prognosis.

No action plan.

Let the news settle.

Frank arrives home. Shaved and sharp and fresh with cold, cloaked in a crombie. His frozen hand reaches out to place itself on my cheek or the back of my neck, make me shiver, jump, laugh, like he did when I was a child. Thinks better of it. Retreats.

'Don't you dare tell him,' she says.

But. It's not the sort of thing you rush to tell your father.

We don't speak much now anyway.

Barbara has grown visibly thinner over the weekend. Is that even possible? While I feel a creeping thickening, imagined or real, around my waist. As if I am eating my mother. Consuming her.

I stay in my room. Cover my body in my biggest sweatshirt, wrap myself in my end-of-bed-blanket, a patched affair, not hand-sewn or any special label, perhaps only a cheap thing, but a relic that lived on the end of Granny's bed. It has long lost her smell, but retains some imagined essence of her.

I sketch. My hand busy over pages of white, giving birth to small detailed pencil faces. From memory. From old and torn photographs, stolen from my mother's albums, stashed in a wooden box under my bed. My mother as a curly-headed serious-eyed child. Granny. Brendan. Grandad. Standing formal in a studio. Proud. Respectable. A family.

I toy with the other items in the box tattooed with my name in faded curlicues, product of a calligraphy set gifted one Christmas when such a thing was in. A hopeful hook-lock ineffectually guarding possessions I consider precious enough to be retained. Diaries, two of them, part-completed. A Barbie outfit, a white ra-ra skirt and pink top. Tiny pink shoes. Letters Fiona sent from the Gaeltacht, when we couldn't afford for me to go. The cat ring from the comic Granny gave me. I kept it for its magic powers. Its ability to protect me from my cousins. *Ha.*

I squeeze the ring on the middle finger of my right hand. I put the stereo on. Fun Boy Three. 'Our Lips Are Sealed.' Start to sway. Start to dance. Escape to the beat. Barbara shouts up the stairs to turn it off. No right to do this now. All privileges revoked. Make no noise. Hide away. Sit at the table. Eat without speaking. Own the guilt. Accept the punishment. What is the punishment? What penance will my mother decide? Grounded. Naturally. I'll take that. The simplicity to think this could be atonement. Time served a fix.

'What will happen? What will we do?' I say.

Throw myself on the mercy of my Stone Guardian. And I'll own a small part of me steals comfort in that we. But. She has no answer.

Frank leaves again. A kiss on both of our heads, remnants of boiled eggs and toast on the table.

I go to school. Walk corridors, carry books, stand in conversation, sit in class. A ghost. Smile when a teacher asks if everything is okay.

'Fine,' I say. 'Just a bit tired.'

Which is all she wants to hear anyway.

Barbara leaves me on Tuesday night with strict instructions, not to go out, not to get into trouble. The word – *trouble* – landing heavy on both of us.

I make tea and butter toast extravagantly and sit in front of the television, pull a blanket around me, sink bare legs deep into safe brown velour. Watch *Blankety Blank, Coronation Street.*

Revel in the ordinariness of it. Contemplate pushing my luck, staying up for *Dynasty* at ten, watch five minutes, turn the television off, go to bed with a hot water bottle. Move the heat of it up and down my body to even the chill from the room. Let it sit on my stomach. Hold it tight. Pray for a miracle.

Half past ten comes and goes. Eleven. Half past eleven.

Frank would often taunt: 'Your mother will be early for her own funeral.'

Midnight. Half-past. She's missed the bus, and the next one, and the next one. None left. Who to call? I don't have a number for Frank. Staying in some bed and breakfast in Salthill, he said. No Galway telephone directory in the house. Not even a name. Brendan and Elena? What could they do, down in Tullamore? Should I call the Guards? My mother's not home, two hours late. Yes, but you don't understand, Guard. Barbara doesn't do this. And, by the way, it's my fault, because I'm pregnant. I'm pregnant. I'm *pregnant*, and I don't know what to do about it and can you please come and take me away now, give my punishment and let this be done. *Get this thing out of me.* Give me my mother back. Give me my ordinary, my stupid worries about exams and hockey practice and who's bitching about who. They'll all be bitching about me soon. My classmates, the neighbours, Brendan and Elena, Sarah, Louisa, Joe. Michael. What will he do?

The door clicks. The sound of stifled shuffling.

'Mammy? Where were you?'

The mother in the hallway is grey and old and unutterably sad. It's in the stoop of her. Movements that crack and creak with pain. Unvarnished white-blue lips breaking skin like pastry left too long to be useful, dried into fissures. A slow hand which unbuttons the good coat, pulls it from broken shoulders, lifts it onto the hook on the wall. Age-crinkled fingers which flex and pat it down tidy. A face that turns, without catching my eye, not a glimmer of life in it.

'Estelle will help us sort it.'

9

Afterwards. The house smells stale, a waft of musk and must that assaults as we walk through the front door. Barbara doesn't move to open windows or the back door. She barely moves at all. As if she is cushioned, bumping gently off the edges of time and reality. I wonder later if Estelle has given her a packet of pills too, the way she passed a supply of Ponstan to me, a white envelope, the measured number of days she expected my pain to last. A hand on my forearm. A tight squeeze.

She underestimated. The bleeding doesn't stop. Not for days and days. A slow heavy drag in my pelvis, disturbing clots. My body, a pregnancy endured if not sustained, behaving as if it has given birth. A shadowy counterfeit, a bagging at my stomach, an ache of milk in my breasts. An ache in my head. A mask clamped tight over my face. No tools for the care of me except Barbara's period pads, huge, with rings on either end for a belt I don't possess. Double knickers going to school.

Can't miss more education.

Leaving Cert.

Focus.

The Future.

Withdraw from Fiona, the others,

cite exams,

cite flu,

cite exhaustion.

Try to remember they have no reason to suspect.

Barbara. Fag-ends in a tray on the smoked-glass coffee table, her legs folded against the chrome frame, so thin they look arty and elegant in the half-light flicker of the soundless television. Her eyes opaque: dead things she takes to work, somehow facilitates function there, brings home again, takes straight to bed. An empty fridge and piles of laundry and dishes in the sink. Me, cleaning up before Frank gets home, cooking spaghetti bolognese, feigning normal, the constant fear he might suspect.

I don't dare complain about the cramps.

But.

'It'll stop soon,' she says.

No eye contact offered.

And I realise she knows this. This. All those times. Those times when babies have fallen from her. Babies she wanted so desperately. And here I am.

A fecund monster.

An aberration.

* * *

She never asks who the father was.

It is, maybe, irrelevant.

In the grim room we shared above a pub in Manchester, nylon bedspreads, noisy plumbing, the blame was mine. When she and Estelle went for food and brought a plate back for me, the blame was mine. Sitting in the order and cleanliness in the clinic, answering questions for a peroxided woman, puffed with lilting tones, the blame was mine. A passive-aggressive constant, which once or twice, when she's home from a gin and orange next door in Kathleen's, erupts into language I didn't realise she knew:

Slut. Whore. Prostitute.

This is what my mother thinks of me.

Perverse.

Her one child is damaged goods. The greatest of failures. Hers. Mine.

* * *

I achieve 27 points in the end. Though they have no idea of the system or the pressure, anything less than perfection is a disappointment to my parents. Straight As are compromised by a B in Honours Maths and a C in Art, justifying the argument that this was a poor subject choice. But. I don't draw anymore. The world has turned grey. I struggle to find colour. I've let my grandmother down, broken my mother. Created and destroyed a child. My child. I am weak and evil and bad and wrong and all those childish words that simply equate to:

NO.

This is what I think of me.

My first choice – Law – is achieved with muted celebration. I arrive in the halls of UCD almost as green as my first day of secondary school. A vague and desperate hope I might meet Michael there. Full of self-loathing. Hating how he still haunts my waking and sleeping hours, how the mention of his name, even on another, can drag me back to that little terraced house in Portobello, the terracotta-coloured sofa, *The Kiss*, the sight of which, a mere mention of Klimt even, sends cortisol running through my veins at breakneck speed. The vain hope, always, that he might trip onto my path, see me across a playing field or in a bar and look at me again the way he looked at me that night. With a seeing I can tell myself is love. A connection so rare and pure and true, it can erase any sin.

This.

A sunk cost fallacy.

Fantasy.

The real Michael is gone long before I arrive, taking with him any imagined absolution.

'Were you offered counselling at the clinic?' the woman says. 'I believe it would have been part of the process. Even at the time.'

Her face is kind.

'I don't think so. I don't know.'

Even now, even here, you can smell that room. The sticky carpet. Badly cleaned food and alcohol stains.

'Estelle might have mentioned something. But she would have said it to my mother.'

'Nobody tried to engage with you directly?'

'Counselling wasn't really an everyday thing then, was it?'

You can't remember details. Only distress.

'I don't think my mother would have believed in it,' you say.

You search your brain for a plausible explanation. You try really hard to find one.

'Maybe she didn't think I deserved it.'

10

May 1990

I am twenty-one. Graduation Day. University College Dublin. Frank and Barbara standing proud either side of me for the obligatory shot by the lake while the photographer pokes his ridiculously long lens in our direction and says things like: 'Brains as well as beauty, eh, love?'

His stomach pouching over low slung corduroy, his pate pink from searing sun refracted off polished concrete and glass.

Early summer posts its promise of long louche evenings as we pose for a class photo, the brightest and the best. Me, with my law degree, my first. And still no hope of a job. But. That's not a worry for today. Today we will go for lunch in the Shelbourne, a tight few of us, and Frank and Barbara will stand awkward with Gerry's parents, tease conservative soundbites about the North and the presidential election, as if they are not entitled to an independent opinion because ... well, they are not barristers themselves.

'Moira is not actually a barrister,' I tell Barbara. 'She's a solicitor – conveyancing, paper-pushing. That sort of thing.'

But such nuance is beyond my mother. Her awe is pathetic and annoying and it underscores a power imbalance between myself and Gerry which is becoming tiresome. Gerry is becoming tiresome. An awkward first date, set up by mutual friends, became a less awkward second date, then an almost-fun third date, and now we are sleeping together for over a year and he is starting to talk saving and starter homes and The Future. He will follow his father to the Bar, of course, he has all the connections. No matter I'm a star of the Literary & Historical society, a renowned debater, would be well able to hold my own in court, I don't come from this world. If I can achieve gainful employment at all, it is likely to be in a firm like his mother's, scrapping for small change from clients with neighbour issues and the vagaries of Will amends. Indeed, Moira has already offered me such industry.

'If you're struggling, Ailish, I'm sure we can organise work experience for you,' she says. Smiling, sweetly.

The woman does not consider me good enough for her boy. And she's probably right. My DNA stands before me. Frank, residually handsome despite the wear now evident in his flesh, still with an eye for a pretty waitress. A middle-aged side-lined civil servant with a fluttering remnant of hope for sexual adventure. Maybe. And Barbara, all prettiness faded to grey. A dress we bought specifically, a salmon pink she liked, considered classy, drains her to a spectre, hangs like loose flesh on her skeletal limbs.

Where on earth do I get my notions?

'You wouldn't ... Gerry's a lovely boy, perfect for you ... you don't need to tell him ... Don't mess it up, Ailish.'

Conversations like this. Stilted. The places Barbara and I can't go. The five-day trip we've erased from our timeline. I don't want to own it any more than she does. I've played the prude, frigid, got a reputation for it. Kept Gerry on a long leash, reeled him in only when he was sure of my virtue. While my classmates danced on tables, drank, dallied with drugs, I paid my penance, kept my head down, made my amends. In summers when other students went travelling, headed off on their J1s, Barbara dragged me to Knock. Took me on pilgrimage to Lough Derg. Lourdes, a highlight, because I got to practise pidgin French and eat croissants.

I watch her now, awkwardly holding a glass of champagne, age thickening and folding her eyelids, narrowing her view, narrowing my view of eyes which let the world in in a different way to mine.

Does she boast about me to Kathleen Dunne next door anymore? Does she say what a wonderful daughter I am, such a good girl? So clever. In UCD. Law, don't you know. My mother's pride in me is muted now. After all, it came before a fall. And maybe this is her take-home message. These days, my mother watches me like I'm made of Semtex, her face implacable, any indication I might have of what goes on behind the façade pure and wild conjecture.

What does my mother think? Does she believe I am damned and all this is an elaborate set-up before an inevitable fall? Or does she believe I am somehow redeemed? Does she believe, behind that high falsetto laugh, that Gerry and his family are forgiveness for our sins, an absolution? Is the reflected glory of

Gerry's father's face, known from newspapers, ruddy with authority, his pronunciation proud with privilege, seen as a sort of exoneration, an answer to her prayers? The Prodigal Daughter, received into the hierarchies of Dublin society and made whole again?

And does she notice, at all, Gerry's father's lecherous palm, his seeking fingers, sliding too far down my back? His saturated pink lips brushing the rim of my ear? Does she fear for me or my defective soul, amongst these people? Does she worry they are *perverse*? She certainly doesn't see me as I see me, outclassed, out of my class, dancing into the arms of a gilded inferno. And if she does, maybe she believes this too is part of our punishment?

But. Maybe shame and recrimination can be forgotten and forgiven here, at least for a while, amongst folded linen and correctly laid cutlery, the costly comfort of plush carpet and silver service.

My mother eats like a bird pecking at the silvered top of a milk bottle. Small disturbances on the plate, a meal sampled, not enjoyed. Frank has no similar qualms. He devours his steak. Eats her creme brûlée as well as his own. Neither of my parents carry weight, the corporeal kind, but something about them, here, in this setting, feels to me excessive, a misplaced decadence, sour, an aura reminiscent of the high sweet fatty smell of fresh milk clotting.

Gerry's parents disturb me in a different way. Embellished decay, perfume and piss, his father fifteen years older than his mother, her beauty now compromised by the slow erosion of menopause, the arrogance of achieving her own definition of success.

This communion of two disparate parts of my life bothers me physically, the heat rising on my neck, my underarms damp, a visceral stickiness. A sudden overwhelm. Nausea. The threat of tears, or suffocation.

'Are you all right, love?' Gerry's father says.

His hand on my upper arm. Brushing my breast.

'I'm fine, Mr Kennedy. Just fine.'

I sit beside my mother. Adjust the skirt of my dress over my knees under the table. Fumble for conversation.

'Wasn't it a lovely ceremony?' I say.

'Pity Brendan and Elena couldn't be here.'

'I could only invite two.'

'They could have come to the lunch.'

I let it sit.

'Oh, did I tell you?' she says. 'Sarah is getting married.'

'Married?'

'Yes. To that Michael fellow. Lovely young man.'

'Michael Hegarty?'

'From up the road, you remember his father bought the Johnson's old farm – you've met him haven't you? He's Joe's friend.'

The words falling like a scythe, a guillotine.

'You're not fine, Ailish love, you've gone completely pale,' Gerry's father says.

His hooded eyes still stuck to me.

'Here, Gerry, take her outside for some air,' he says. 'She looks like she's about to pass out.'

11

The months wear on and the pressure for us to go to the wedding as a family is immense. It's there in the outsized graduation photograph sitting on the sideboard, alongside a trophy Frank won in a golf competition, some unspecified time ago. Me. An achievement. A daughter completed, like a piece of knitting. Barbara keen now to show off her handiwork. The next stop on the conveyor belt, a finish line, maybe, in sight.

Gerry wants to go too.

'I'd love to meet your extended family,' he says. 'You've met all mine.'

And I have. I've been paraded at dinners and christenings and corporate events. I've agonised over the right outfit for the specific occasion, unsure of labels and brands and trends, hoping dresses from Next would be good enough, splashing out on Pamela Scott, money saved hard from my lounge girl job in the pub up the road.

Got it right. Got it wrong.

'Aren't those earrings lovely,' Moira says. 'Fabulous for a night out.'

When we are at a charity lunch one day. More like this. Insidious, evanescent, untraceable little barbs, picking away at the boundaries of me. Trying to erase me bit by bit. My uncertain pedigree hovering around me like a malodourous aura.

* * *

Sarah is the first of this generation to walk down the aisle and Brendan is under pressure, Elena an enthusiastic Mother of the Bride. The phone zings with news. A Christmastime wedding. New Year's Eve, better yet. Even if I were to get a job, I wouldn't be able to claim I couldn't get time off. And I have no money to go anywhere else. The only option seems to be to feign sickness, which may take little acting skill.

I pluck my way through October and November, CVs and application forms, idle of proper work and more or less penniless, the bar-work pittance plus tips not enough to keep up with Gerry's lifestyle. My head lost in complexity. Finding my fledgling adult feet amidst Barbara's chatter and excitement about Sarah's Big Day, a pulling to life that I'm grateful for, but a tentative request to be a bridesmaid which is answered with an emphatic '*No*'. I picture my brain as a ball of elastic bands, the outer ones ready to snap, the inner ones so tangled they can never be unpicked. Criss-crossing connections of rubber so tight and messed up it hurts.

As the days shorten dramatically, I'm adrift. Missing college.

The structure and support of it. The mental challenge. A few of us had enthusiastically formed our own debating society, met in the M1 a few times, but we lacked focus and easy access to alcohol derailed us. The days in Theatre L are over, and I realise now how I had used this outlet, this formal application of logic to affairs of human frailty, to balance myself. A vent for pent-up anger. A point well made with wit, the annihilation of an opponent, not only food for my ego, a blood-letting, a lifeline.

They didn't expect it of me. The world in general. I didn't expect it of me. I am still slight and fair and pretty in a quiet unnoticeable way, but a well-phrased motion can set me off on a path of argument that will make well-built jocks and committed nerds quake. I can feel myself lit. A power. Know that there's a sexual edge to it. Know this is what keeps Gerry in tow, that there are others interested if I want them. And sometimes I do. But I don't. I'm demure as a nun in my Levi jeans and Adidas trainers, my grandfather shirt buttoned tight. Glasses an accessory of the past, thanks to new-fangled contact lenses. I can argue a passionate libertarian diatribe about divorce and abortion and women's rights, cheerlead for change and contraception and the new president, but when it comes down to it I'm still Ailish McCarthy of 16 Bellevue Drive.

Bland, ordinary, repressed.

A Good Girl.

This is why Gerry likes me. An educated woman who will fit with his parents' public persona, a confidence I will ultimately crew for his captaincy, become a paper-pusher like his mother, raise his children, charitably help unfortunates who have made mistakes because I can rationalise their situation intellectually.

I am steeped in extraordinary compassion for 'the other'.

I am 'the other'.

* * *

The void in my stomach is a constant. Sometimes it escapes me, spreads to engulf the world in a cloud, drains it. I don't want a baby. Have never wanted a baby, never seriously contemplated it for a moment, but some days I am obsessed. They are everywhere, these women with bulbous stomachs struggling to balance on stick legs, pushing prams and go-cars with snot-nosed toddlers, cotton-and-wool pastel-clad infants I ache to pick up and smell. I don't want a baby. But. I wonder if mine would have Michael's lips. My eyes. Would it be bald or one of those hairy babies, soft-fluff-powdered luminous strands you could bury your nose in, trail along your cheek? Brush light against your eyelids. Inhale. A boy or a girl? A girl to dress like a little doll, one of the pink-and-white outfits which trip me up in Dunnes when I look for a suitable Christmas present for Barbara. Of which there are none.

We stopped going to Tullamore for Christmas the year of The Trip To England. We celebrate it in Dublin now, the three of us, chicken and congealed gravy, over-boiled sprouts, Paxo stuffing, Penney's three-for-two presents. Socks, hankies and deodorant. Frank made no argument when Barbara first said she wanted to stay home, like a star-crossed lover might, and I wondered if I'd misconstrued the situation between himself and

Elena. Maybe there was no scandal, no affair, no great love between my father and my aunt. Maybe all those glances and innuendo meant nothing. Maybe it was only in *my* head. And, somehow, rather than find comfort in this thought, it makes me sad. If my father isn't the glamorous Lothario I'd imagined, who is he? An ordinary middle-aged man skirting both sides of the country looking for succour, for connection, for peace? Sitting faded and lonely in a bar somewhere hoping someone might take a fleeting interest in his all-too-common story of an attempted family, a wife he tried to support, a daughter he doesn't know now. Somebody who might tether him for a little while. Make him believe there is magic.

He will tell me later, much later, in a fit of demented reminiscence: 'Your mother was very beautiful when we met, you know. Full of fun.'

But while I can imagine her having being pretty once, the Barbara I've known rarely cracks a smile. Bears no resemblance to my father's narrative.

12

We arrive to an infestation of Elena's people, the farmhouse in fiesta mode, the feel of it foreign, changed. The wedding, New Year's Eve, is two days away, but the party is already flying, the kitchen brimful of loud jabbering Spaniards, bloated from Christmas, jostling with over-pronounced vowels and angsty hands. Puffs of Channel and Paco Rabanne and primary colours. Glitz and glorified tendrils of hair, women and men equally polished and buffed. The pungent whiff of loosened social norms.

'Ailish, *chica*, you've met my sister Penelope?' Elena says.

Penelope, a younger and even more beautiful version of Elena, comes complete with a clatter of offspring, early versions of my cousins, who will be flower children. They mope, huddled in jumpers, complaining bitterly of the cold. The smallest, Theodora, four, maybe five, takes a shy shine to me.

I'm having none of it.

'Ailish isn't used to children,' my mother says.

Apologetically. As if this is a mere by-the-by, a shallow lifestyle choice.

Barbara is sparkly high, an aura of anxiety I picture wrought into finely woven threads of glass. Frank and I exchange wary glances, keep an eye on where she is, watch for an off-beat, alert to what she is saying. What she is drinking. She's not a big drinker. A badly timed glass of wine could do for her, awaken carefully nurtured slights, erode the fragile mortar holding her together, turn the carefully curated tableau to dust.

We are staying in the farmhouse, Elena's cousin Jose and his family have been ejected especially to accommodate us, doubtless resulting in a lot of enthusiastic Mediterranean bitching, which my mother is oblivious to. Would be even if she spoke their language.

'We were so sorry we couldn't make it for Christmas,' she says. To anybody not quick enough to escape her. 'But Ailish's boyfriend, Gerry, his mother and father, they were having us over for St Stephen's Day. Huge big affair. They live on Aylesbury Road, you know. Charlie was there.'

This last an octave lower, her mouth action over-pronounced. As if imparting dangerous information. As if they might be impressed. Know that 'Charlie' is the Taoiseach. Know, even, what a taoiseach is. A hopeful validation of me, her, an unnecessary trinket to underscore the desirability of our presence.

'It's all about degrees of connection in Ireland, don't you know,' I say apologetically. Raise my eyebrows in an attempt to disown her.

I'm in my usual room. But it is a room I have not usually been in for years now. A ghost of child-me sits on the bed playing with her Barbies. Dressing them and fixing their hair:

the blonde, an aspirational future Ailish, the dark-haired one, maybe, Sarah. A strappy, spotty, summer dress for me, neat hair tied back. A single strand of plait, an off-the-shoulder top and skirt, for her. The pair of them heading into the world, young women on the cusp, living independently in a kitchen crafted from cardboard, a bed made from a book. Working, glamorously, in offices. Dating. A Hawaiian-shirt-clad Ken and Joe's discarded Action Man. Hanging out together, telling each other all our secrets. Wordless play in the hours when I could legitimately hide here, hide in my head, the pressure to mingle and be seen relieved because adults were busy.

I sit on the familiar bedspread, the patches and threads of it hurtling me back in time. It is rumoured to have been made by my grandmother's mother, coveted in my childhood by my own mother, designated a family heirloom, morally hers. When the time came to claim it, she didn't have the energy, couldn't place it in our three-bed semi. Too rustic. She cast it aside and gave focus to the bigger insult, the fate of the farm. Memories of lying here, after my grandmother died. My mother's compound and complex grief. Her ill-hid disappointment.

'Five thousand pounds?'

'You knew Brendan was inheriting the farm.' my father said.

'But a lousy five thousand pounds? And Sarah and Louisa get my grandmother's rings? Ailish gets a watch? I'm the eldest, Frank. It's not fair.'

But that was Before. Barbara Before cared about such things. Barbara Before was an Innocent, a victim of cruel circumstance, robbed of inheritance because of her gender, robbed of her babies by a body that refused its biological imperative, robbed of the comfortable middle-class life she thought she was entitled to by a feckless and ineffectual husband. A straightforward narrative. Black and white. Wrong and right.

Barbara now is Barbara After. Barbara After lives in a world of mist and grey edges. Barbara After is a Sinner. Hoist by her own petard. Has committed, in her own opinion, through an act of procurement, the ultimate evil. The termination of a life. It's a story she cannot own on any conscious level. A story her subconscious rails against. She blames me, loves me, hates me, sees me as a prodigal. Her job to ensure I achieve atonement. Reparation. When she kneels in church and prays, her reptile brain feverishly negotiates a deal with her God. If she can deliver me to him whole, chastened, repentant, then maybe we will both be saved.

Of course, this is conjecture.

But.

I think I'm not wrong.

However.

It's wearing thin on me.

This mantle of shame.

* * *

The three of us are quickly ensconced, slipping into a familiar routine, ingrained ways of being with the others. Barbara all scarcely contained disapproval; Frank full of bonhomie; me, quiet. Gerry is coming down on the day of the wedding. I've been putting him off, which is easy now he's a trainee in his father's firm.

'Couldn't get time off even over Christmas,' I tell my mother. 'He's that important.'

Sarkiness wasted, the negative of his absence morphing quickly to a positive she can utilise in conversation. A gift to distract her. I can't imagine him here, in the farmhouse, with near wild dogs and cats sniffling at his ankles, the smell of cooking and underlying damp.

I have a recurrent nightmare, almost every night now, where I find myself at a huge Dublin party, walking naked through crowds, struggling to find a face I know. All of them wearing the right clothes, knowing the right thing to say. The right accents. Me, opening my mouth to reveal flat elongated vowels and dropped Gs that never belonged to me. Searching the throng for an Offaly jersey.

Since the wedding announcement, I find I quietly absent myself from conversations, from my physical location, and go searching my memory and my imagination for Michael. A Michael who was, is, and might never be. Examining the dusty wormholes of my brain like an archaeologist for the tiniest trace … of what I don't know. Resolution? Salvation?

Some ever-elusive version of peace.

* * *

The house is oppressive with preparation. Small with sheathed clothes and shoes and beaded finery finding home in unsuitable places. Noisy with excitement and rows. Sarah, at the epicentre, is twenty-four now. Her beauty at its peak. An effortless grace, coupled with a capacity for kindness that might suck you in, kill you on the turn. I watch her endlessly. Carefully. Careful not to be caught. I can hear the '*She was always odd, creeps me out*' upon potential discovery, but I'm helpless to resist the swerves of her, the curves, the elegance. Simple tasks like blow-drying her hair or putting on lipstick might be a symphony. The studied competence when she paints her nails, a work of art in itself.

Louisa, well, she has got fatter. Each extra pound making her exponentially less gainly. Tullamore blood rising high on Spanish skin turning it country. Something has turned within her also, as if she has already abandoned hope of a life she wished to have. The air of somebody who has made a largely unsatisfactory treaty with truth. A settling incongruent with her years.

'You've given up the nursing?' I say.

Conversationally, picking at the heap of lunch food Elena has laid on the kitchen table, my stomach hopping with nerves, a kind of horrified hope, the constant possibility here that the door might open. That it might be Michael.

'Yeah, they were awful bitches, the nuns,' she says. 'Treated us like servants. Then Ronan offered me the job in the office and, like, you know, it was a no-brainer.'

Ronan is her boyfriend. Local estate agent, unprepossessing type, also rotund. Balding. Shiny. She has told me, confidentially, flatly, they are to be engaged. She's waiting for

Sarah's wedding to be over before making an announcement. He seems equally unenthusiastic, the only spark in him visible when his roundy eyes narrow to contemplate property.

'Great move, this marriage, y'know,' he says. 'Like I know Joe will take over the farm, but Brendan is talking about giving Sarah the top field, right beside that land Michael's parents have in for rezoning. You could fit three hundred houses between the two, y'know.'

His words slow and pronounced, because, maybe, I am ignorant to these ways of the world.

Y'know.

I walk through the rooms, up and down the stairs, like a woman-child condemned. Joe's ghost of yore made flesh. Sarah and Louisa are full of chatter, friendly in an offhand way. In their reality I'm only a bit player. An extra.

'So is this Gerry good-looking?' Sarah says.

'He's nice,' I say.

'Barbara seems to like him.'

'She does.'

'Sounds like he's loaded.'

I shrug.

'You've turned into a bit of a ride yourself,' Louisa says.

'She's right, you know, you're lovely looking,' Sarah says.

A considered gaze. My entire body tingles. I imagine her eyes linger a little too long. A frantic scattering of secrets searching for cover.

'Thanks.'

And then too quickly:

'Where's Michael?'

I blush, as if I have, and maybe I have, subconsciously linked my – increased? – physical attractiveness with his presence? But it's out there. The question I've wanted to ask all day.

'Oh, he's with the lads tonight,' Sarah says. 'Joe said something about Loughrey's. Mama's having this hen-do in the house for all the auld biddies in Tullamore. She did tell you and Barbara about it?'

'She did,' I say.

'Yeah, well. I guess I won't see him now until the altar.'

Which I guess means I won't see him either, now, until the altar.

13

Gerry arrives to a cacophony of wedding angst. Like an alien landed, his Louis Copeland suit in a monikered bag, swung over a rugby-honed shoulder. As with all men, Elena tries to flirt, and through his lens I see my impossibly gorgeous aunt-by-marriage turn into a sun-beaten middle-aged try-hard. As if her glow has been sanded down, buried under too many layers of paint.

Louisa realised yesterday that her bridesmaid dress no longer fit. If it ever had at all. An aspirational buy, the dream of dropping a size now smoke. The shops were shut. Her debs dress – the wrong colour, but hanging ready in plastic – two sizes smaller again. A frantic scurry in Elena's scrap odds and ends produced nothing that could be employed in a fix. A curtain from a spare room was recruited, sacrificed, added to the back of the dress in a complex negotiation of Singer sewing machine and zip. On either side now runs a slice of brocade which almost matches the carefully chosen forest-green silk. Her confidence and humour are in shreds.

She has set herself up doing make-up for those who want it

in the dining room. Elena's sisters, some of the Spanish cousins, queue. Wrapped in a white towelling dressing gown, her hair in curlers, Louisa decorates her kin, makes them beautiful, seeming to grow increasingly uncomfortable in her own skin, each additional request less time for her to get ready herself. When it comes to the bride, finally out of the bath, her patience has worn threadbare.

'Oh, sit still, for fuck's sake,' she says.

I watch Elena watching with a nervous eye her youngest daughter ceding the stage once more to her older sister with ill grace born of conflicting emotion. She loves her sister. She hates her sister. She wants to be her sister. It's hard to be Louisa.

'Calm down,' Sarah says. 'You'll take my eye out. It's not all about you.'

'No, well, it never is, is it? I'm just a lackey whose sole purpose in life is to wait on you – isn't that the truth of it?'

More like this. The room is a swirl of colours: pinks, oranges, reds. Decibels rising. Brendan arrives, his unrufflable demeanour ruffled. Shouts at Louisa. Calms Sarah. Louisa storms from the room. Elena runs after her, brings her back. Sobs. Negotiations. Temporarily covered cracks.

I do my own make-up.

* * *

And here we are. The church is wide, almost semi-circular, modern. Pews with tan leatherette kneelers, an awkward shuffle of shoe and shin around baseboard.

The burgundy Laura Ashley velvet dress I bought in Oxfam fits snug to my curves. The hat Barbara insisted I wear – black felt, cloche-shaped – feels awkward, but, I am told, suits me. Frames my face, makes my fair features more distinct. Gerry likes it. Is attentive, complimentary, senses that my head is elsewhere. Maybe.

Joe and Helen sit in front. They are living in a flat in town now, living together, living in sin. It's a subject of some judgement. Still uncommon, pass-remarkable.

'He'll never marry her,' Barbara said as we were walking into the church. Me forging ahead to avoid her continuous commentary on events. Her mouth tiny with disapproval.

'Why do you say that?' I said.

'If you're getting the milk for free why would you buy the cow?'

'Oh, for God's sake. You're still living in the Dark Ages. Is it not more stupid to get married and then decide you can't stand the other person's snoring or leaving their nail-clippings around or whatever? At least they know what they're getting into.'

I do this now. Claw at the locks. Argue. A liberal viewpoint can send her into a spasm. I do it deliberately. I do it with malice aforethought. I do it despite the potential consequences. I do it for the potential consequences. I am exhausted avoiding explosions. I need an explosion. I want to blow it all up.

'Gerry and I are considering it,' I said.

Knowing how it will land. Neurons darting like fireworks across her brain.

'Considering what?'

'Living together.'

'You're not serious.' Her eyes wide under her hat, every fibre of her alert. 'Gerry wouldn't ...'

'Would he not?'

'Ailish, you can't, have you not done enough damage ...'

'Relax, Mother, I'm joking.'

* * *

I sit, bold eyes boldly ahead for the show. The four of us lined up and rigid. Frank, like an artful line drawing, all colour faded. Barbara, extra stiff now and watchful. Gerry, trying to channel an 'I can fit anywhere' politician vibe, when, really, he can't. Every fibre of me on alert, conscious of the band on the hat, where it sits on my hair, on my head, the lining of my dress slippery on my tights, my thighs, my waist and breasts strained to the cloth of the bodice. My hands skim the pile of the fabric smooth on my hip bones, clutch at my bag, knead it.

At the altar, Michael stands. His brother Eamonn, his best man, at his side. They are sharing some in-joke, heads inclined, shoulders shifting nervously. The back of his neck is tidy with fresh-cut stubble, scrubbed.

I wonder has he thought of me at all. Maybe, knowing that I would be there, he avoided the house deliberately. It might be awkward, or painful, for him.

Ha.

The thought whirls and rankles. This man has played such a huge part in my story, am I in his at all? Apart from that night, he has only ever barely acknowledged me. Never tried to contact me – never for a second, as far as I know, given a passing thought to my welfare. I could be one of many sideline indiscretions. He might be the type of man who cheats habitually, rationalises it, justifies it, moves on without it touching him. It was simply a moment of madness, when he was cross with Sarah, looking for a substitute, a night of confusion. A twinge of regret, no more.

But.

What if, as in my fevered imaginings, he has watched me grow from afar, as I have watched him, was caught unawares that night in Portobello, swept up in feelings so strong he lost sight of rationality. Has churned and yearned ever since, unable to act because of the Mannions, because he has let too much time pass now, because, because ... This is the genre of my go-to-narrative and, though I know why this is, how unlikely the veracity of it, I am continually drawn to excuse him. He might have been thwarted. He might be contracted in some unholy way by his parents, standing there now: a farm-heavy woman, his mother, in florals – his father, fingers puffed from manual work and drinking. Simple people. Like Uncle Brendan, but different. Subsistence people. In thrall to the like of the Mannions. Uncle Brendan's Range Rover and milking parlours, his meticulous calculation of quotas and EEC grants. Maybe this is a marriage of economy ...

But.

The music starts.

I turn my head.

All my dreams are blown to tiny colour-bright shards.

In her wedding dress Sarah is breathtaking. Raw silk skimming tanned shoulders, tight to the waist. Curls artfully escaping her bun, the veil, falling softly on the precise construction of her neck. Neat pointed shoe-tips peeping from a full skirt. A Disney Princess come to life.

Brendan walks his smiling daughter up the aisle to the heartbreaking sight of Michael's side profile, soft and nervous in response,

smiling and

in love.

I forget to breathe.

Inhale sharply.

Exhale.

A sound that translates almost as a sob.

* * *

I have played this wedding out in fantasy a million times over. Adjusted the script, the lighting, the setting, the sound, as Barbara, oblivious, channelled new titbits of information my way.

'Lilies. In her bouquet. I thought lilies were for funerals. Is that a Spanish thing, d'you think?'

'A DJ, not a band.'

'The Bridge House. Nearly three hundred guests. Thank God Brendan has pots of money, that's going to cost a fortune.'

'A harpist in the church. Did you ever?'

'One bridesmaid, but *six* flower girls and pageboys.'

Small details, insignificant, brushstrokes on a canvas, creating a picture in my head. The bits I added myself.

Originally:

I'd imagined it in the farmhouse. Our first meeting, the first time to lay eyes on each other, since. Before the wedding. A family meal. Looks. Longing. Mutual. An accidental-on-purpose encounter in the yard. Moonlit. Eyes connecting, hands brushing.

Adjustment:

Our first meeting. In the church, as I take my place three pews behind. Him turning.

Eyes connecting. Knowing. Truth.

'Do you take this woman ...?' the priest would say.

'I don't. I can't,' he might say.

His voice choked with realisation, emotion.

Adjustment:

The first time I see him in the flesh, since, is here, here and now, and here and now he can. Here and now, he can take this woman. Here and now, he does. He takes this woman with delight, a whoop of encouragement, of joy, rippling through the congregation.

'You can clap if you like,' says the priest.

And they do. As Michael kisses his bride, they cheer. As he walks her down the aisle, they forget they are in a church at all. Some even whistle. And he whistles past me. Without so much as a look.

* * *

Mulled wine and jewelled colours and Christmas tree twinkles. Spotlights. Hairspray. Perfume. The heady sweet sweat of hangover. Laughter. Young flesh mixing with tired mixing with old. Elena's mother, wheelchair-bound, staying at the hotel in the care of Elena's older sister, Ana. Careworn, mannish. At the hen-do, she got drunk on malt whiskey, cried more than necessary.

Gerry, puffed, more at home here than the worn contours of the farmhouse. A visible relaxing. As if aged, scrubbed wood and uneven edges are an offense to him. As if fitted carpet, marble and brass are his birthright.

'I haven't introduced myself to the groom yet,' he says.

I steer him towards Ronan, the price of farm acreage. Louisa is fraying at the eyes, tears threatening to erupt, held back by a plastic smile. She's uncomfortable in her girth. Seeking comfort in Prosecco. I smile sympathy, but it lands suspicious. I feel a pang for a relationship we simply don't have.

Elena conducts operations with her eyes. Darting this way and that, wolfishly alert, sweeping the room for an idle serving girl, simultaneously engaging with her family, switching effortlessly from Spanish to English, toothy smile to instructional nod. Her dress is magnificent, royal-blue gauze, plumb cut to impressive cleavage.

Brendan carries his farm-worn body, muscles overdeveloped from necessity, limbs carved through toil, through the room with heavy relief. Each footfall deliberate. Each smile earned. Bestowed with meaning.

Joe and Helen, casually engaged in proceedings, ideologically aloof, holding court with contemporaries. Her smile is stuck, a rictus exhausted from effort, I think. To let it fall at all an admission. She's giving the milk for free and making out like it doesn't matter.

Children running everywhere untamed, puffed-silk skirts and forest-green sashes, patent leather shoes. Uncomfortable trousers, restrictive waistcoats, the raw wild freedom of newly shorn locks. Crashing into chairs, crawling under tables, high on sugar. High on life.

The little girl, Theodora, chased by a boy cousin, falls back onto Barbara's sensible shoe, her bunion. Awakening a different Barbara. A guttural yelp, an automatic quickening – in both of us. A hand raised.

'*Mum!*'

My voice hanging high in the air, solidifying and splintering, like craquelure spreading on fine porcelain.

She looks at me, disconnected. Drunk. On wine or madness or both.

'It'll be you next,' she says.

Ignoring her injury, the neighbours stand next to her, drinks halted midway to their mouths.

'I'm not getting married for a long time, Mum,' I say. 'Maybe not ever.'

* * *

At the bar, Frank is getting a pint in. And a chaser.

'I'll have a gin and tonic,' I tell him.

We stand, jostled either side, arms touching. The first touch in years. The same blood running through us, the same discomfort, seeking the same fix.

'Sarah looks well all the same.'

'She does.'

'Is your mother ...?'

'She's okay, Dad. Just need to ...'

'I'll ...'

'It's okay.'

'Are you not getting one for Gerry?'

'He's fine.'

'Ah here, get the fella a pint, for God's sake.'

He motions to the barman, who slots another glass under a pump, a practised movement, brown liquid caressing the smooth surface, darkening to black. The ritual settling. Frank picks up the pint to take to Gerry and I follow, for want of any better option.

Gerry, who has located, and is talking to, Michael.

I feel sick. Sweaty.

'I have a friend who did Ag Science, he's saying, same as yourself. Got a job with the EU now, off out in Brussels. Forty grand a year. Peter Tierney, you didn't come across him? Probably a couple of years below you.'

Michael is shaking his head.

As I approach, we catch each other's eye. I've played and replayed this as an imagined moment so many times. A look, a zing, a spark, words without words, connection, understanding, meaning ...

I get: recognition.

'Hi, Ailish,' he says.

Smiling.

Polite.

As if I am ... Joe's little cousin, back at the funeral, sipping lemonade, feeling sad.

As if that was the last time he saw me.

I nod back.

'Congratulations,' I say.

The word floating out so naturally.

'Thanks.'

Sarah is at his side. Smiling. Beautiful. Ethereal.

'Congratulations,' I say.

'Thanks, Ailish. My feet are only fucking killing me in these shoes – they've practically sliced my little toes right off.'

Only I notice Gerry's slight intake of breath. Small judgement on the bridal swearword. A minute recalibration of me and my people.

Only I seem to float metaphorically high above the scene, recognise its significance, or insignificance, swirling, melding colourfully into courteous chitchat. The groom and his bride laughing, distracted, sucked up into the throng.

Only I.

Only me.

Standing there, a mess of barely contained atoms. Flanked by Frank and Gerry.

Barbara loose in the room.

'It was a difficult week.'

'How so?'

'Tuesday would have been her birthday.'

'You found it hard?'

Breathe.

'I'm a bit flat. Weary, I guess.'

'Did you mark it?'

'I took Frank to the grave. Just the two of us.'

'How was that?'

An image of the grave before you. The wind. The churn in your stomach.

'Odd. Like I was bringing him to visit his past and his future.'

'Was he aware?'

'It's hard to say, isn't it? Hard to know how much of him is left. Sometimes there's a glimpse, you know?'

'You did the right thing, marking the day.'

'Did I? I don't know it brought him any comfort.'

'Not for him. For you.'

'The strange thing is, we were never really big on celebrating birthdays.'

14

October 1995

Claire and David are having a dinner party. They're engaged and have bought a four-bed in Booterstown, a starter home, a doer-upper. David's dad has given them a sizeable chunk of the deposit and Claire's parents are paying for the wedding. I'm surprised to get an invite, even more surprised I accepted. But. October is long, I'm curious, and it will get Fiona off my back about getting out more. Claire and I work together, intersecting friend groups, friendly, but not close. I suspect she has an application in for promotion and is 'relationship building'. These are the machinations of law firms. Or perhaps she simply needs even guest numbers for etiquette.

There are eight of us. Two other couples and a friend of David's from work. One of those awkward obvious set-up situations. David is cooking. His job is notedly stressful, something highflying in tech. Household chores – cooking, gardening, DIY – help him relax, Claire says. She is full of apologies for the unfinished state of the house, lengthy explanations of their plans to extend, then move in five or ten years, when, inevitably, they will have several children and outgrow the space. The table, an inheritance from a grandmother, an antique name I don't recognise, dropped randomly, is set for a minutely orchestrated casual supper – candlelight, everyday Denby, weighty Jerpoint glasses.

It's Friday night. I was at my desk at seven-thirty this morning and worked through until six. On a coveted solicitor training contract even leaving at six on a Friday raises a cold eyebrow. My ablutions were rushed. My hair is still damp. I am wearing a dress I bought down a side street on holiday in Lisbon. Black, embroidered and beaded. Opaque tights and black kitten heels.

Claire hands me a glass of Chardonnay, ushers me to one of two overstuffed sofas set either side of the fire, dominating the modest proportions of the room.

'I'm sure you and Gerry will hit it off,' she says. 'He's such a great guy. Just through a bad break-up, you know. An awful rip.'

The name resonates. Gerry and I have hardly spoken since we split, but I'm aware through the tenuous pre-social-media network of things, that he has been long-term dating an Amanda from Mount Merrion, who, though I've never met the girl, sits in my head as blonde and pretty and posh, a me with the bona fides to please his mother. If that is feasible. I've not heard they have broken up. Of course, it might be another Gerry, but Dublin is small, this sort of set even smaller. I'm aware of the damp hair, the thrown-on make-up. The potential need to put on a show for my ex. I excuse myself to the cramped downstairs bathroom, make what reparations I can with a cracked compact and remnants of a lipstick. Wonder why I am nervous. Decide it is about maintaining face. Wonder if it is too late to make my excuses and head home.

* * *

Home is Merrion Square, a top floor flat, which is a trudge with groceries, but feels safe from the post-dark pimp and prostitute activities on the street. I've only once had an incident, a man high on drugs accosting me at the door, and he was more disoriented than dangerous. Having Niall as a flatmate helps, if purely from the perspective of his gender and height, and the sub-let mate's rates rent he offers is competitive. I serve a purpose for him also, a smokescreen for curious onlookers in the law firm where he works. A distraction from the throng of men who file through our kitchen, drink my coffee, eat my bread.

'For fuck's sake, Niall, you're a complete slut,' I say.

In the grip of realising-I-have-nothing-to-toast angst.

'Did you catch that guy's name?' he says.

'I did not. Why are you worried? It's not like you're going to see him again.'

'*Hmmm* ...'

'You need to be more careful, you know. You'll literally catch your death.'

'I'm careful. I'm clean. Don't worry, baby.'

He kisses me on the forehead. A brotherly kiss, a half-hug which brings a lump to my throat, because I love him. And I worry about him. His vulnerability in a world which drips judgement and danger. All his secrets.

The flat is home in a way home never was. Comfortable carpet and corduroy-covered sofas at an angle, a coffee table sprawled with art books, magazines. Bookshelves, mostly Niall's, but my collection is growing. Economically framed prints – Van Gogh, Monet, Manet – line the hallway return from the door to our eyrie. The generous landing sports a cheeky collection of prints of Picasso etchings, Niall's small collection of originals, Sunday shopping on Merrion Square acquisitions, his own life-sketches, all men, which are rather good.

I don't draw any more, bar the odd doodle on a legal pad, but since moving here I've turned domestic. When I finish work I come home and clean the fridge. Scour the bath, rub furiously at marks that won't bleach. I knit. I sew and I cook. Grow basil in a pot. An escape from days slaving over contracts, toiling with words to ensure their meaning is interpreted in a particular way. Or not. The open kitchen shelves laden with our collection of spices excites me. I tear recipes from *The Sunday Times* magazine, invite friends over to complement and compliment my creativity. To indulge lofty ideas and ideals in the decreasing maturity of semi-pretentious wine.

I will remember these as days of quiet contentment. Fulfilment. Autonomy. Hope. But under the surface, mounting pressure. Couplings and weddings. The imperative to reproduce mounting. With every baby announcement, I feel a tug. A ghost infant stalking me, throwing shade at my notions of independence. It's viability. Desirability.

Fiona, a doctor now, is having none of it.

'The nuclear family is purely a social construct, born of economic necessity,' she says.

As we sit, feet propped on the coffee table, cotton wool between our toes, Chanel Rouge Noir bleeding into untrimmed clefts of skin. Tissues stained murderous red resting lightly on *Vogue, Cosmopolitan, Marie Claire*.

'A man isn't necessary to have a baby. Mum and I were perfectly fine when Dad left. Better.'

And maybe they were. Yvonne is still a powerhouse, a formidable woman. The mother of my friend, but also my friend. Kind and wise and pragmatic. A juxtaposition to Barbara. To Frank.

I think about them as little as I can now, because to do so is uncomfortable. Unproductive. Since I moved out, Barbara's lapses have become more frequent. Different. Darker. Plumbing a well of ever-decreasing hope. Various pills, fixes, suggested, not working. Frank walking blankly through it, prisoner of a gold band around his finger, his wallet, his life, titrating Xanax and Valium like an alchemist, his own sanity blinking in the obsession of maintaining hers.

I take the bus home on Sundays, a night during the week if work permits.

Yvonne is a comfort, supports this strategy of benign neglect.

'You'll only ever scratch the surface, darling,' she says. 'Your mother is on her own journey. You need to mind yourself.'

But how much of the fault is mine? And then, to exonerate me, to allow me to function, I think: how much of the fault is

Frank's? Surely he has some skin in this game of guilt. Surely it's not all my fault?

* * *

When he sees me, Gerry's face lights up. And I recognise in a rush how it is such a kind face, all semi-receding hair and angles. Already crinkly eyes.

'You look well,' he says.

'So do you.'

'You two know each other?' Claire says.

'We were in college together,' I say.

He smiles. A small conspiracy.

'Ah, Dublin is tiny,' she says. 'Everybody knows everybody. That's great.'

'It is,' I say. 'Great.'

And I feel a warmth and ease I haven't felt for a long time. A comfort in the simple presence of Gerry I hadn't realised I'd missed. For all my celebration of the single state, there's a window on the past here to a space where I knew the rules, a steady place, where norms were set and adhered to. Generally.

We'd limped along for a year or so after Sarah and Michael's wedding. Twin pressures: Barbara's head obsessed with sealing the deal, a wedding of her own. Mine – still obsessed with Michael, his indifference, which I couldn't reconcile, no matter how I tried to logic it out. The finality of him being married didn't seem to alleviate my feelings. If anything, it added to the frustration.

In the end, the decision to call it off was almost mutual. Time and space needed. He wanted to travel, go to America, Australia, Thailand, see the world. I couldn't afford it.

'Not even backpacking?' he'd said.

Not even that.

I'd fancied his reaction was relief.

I flailed around at home for six months after he left. Played heartbroken to avoid Barbara's blame, felt guilty when she was kind. She naturally assumed it was Gerry I was grieving, doled out comfort. I lay in bed, unemployed, unloved, tearstained. She lay an awkward hand on my shoulder, patted it, brought me food, solaces from my childhood, a milk-and-bread-and-sugar concoction from her life on the farm she called 'goodie'. It slid down my throat like it was all the wholesomeness in life itself.

Eventually, I could lie there no longer. I got a job, moved out, moved on. The wrench was brutal.

'How's your mum?' Gerry says now.

The clink of plates and glasses and cutlery, as we sit stiffly side by side.

'Ah, you know. Still Barbara.'

He nods. A resigned air which tells me I don't need to explain further. We already have this shorthand.

* * *

I've dated three guys since our split. All Dublin 4 stereotypes, privately educated rugby heads, for these are the men who come across my path. I slept with only the first. An enthusiastic wine-fuelled release, which led to a 'You're very good at this' shaming in thin morning light, his cut-price bobbled duvet-set a grubby witness to my mortification. After that, I was wary. Subsequent dates chaste. A growing conclusion this is a game I am useless at.

The dinner table conversation flits between the Rugby World Cup, the tenuous peace process and the divorce referendum.

Gerry is surprisingly passionate on the subject. 'We can't market ourselves as a first world country, pitch for foreign direct investment if we're stuck in the pocket of the Church,' he says. 'How can we attract Europeans to work in Microsoft, Intel, if we've no legal infrastructure in place to support them in their personal lives? No room for error. No divorce, no abortion?'

As always, the word itself hits high, a wolfish invasion in my head. The 'divorce' word hits too – for who, if it were legal, if it were feasible, would be better candidates than my parents? A shivery thought. Barbara, abandoned. Mine.

'Abortion is entirely different,' David says.

'Is it not a question of the right to self-determination? The same as divorce?' I say.

'Well, divorce is about two adult people. It's about putting in place a legal framework for them to move on, to make sure children are looked after, for any combined assets to be divided fairly. It's sad, but it's a mechanism for ending a relationship. Abortion is about ending a life. It's entirely different.'

'It's about the right to autonomous decision-making on matters affecting your own life,' I say. 'I would argue in that way it's exactly the same. They're both human rights issues.'

'What about the human rights of the child?'

'What about the rights of the woman?'

My voice is rising. Muscle memory from my debating days kicking into gear, taking in the faces around the table focused on mine, some engaging, some deserting me. It's a distasteful subject, more suited to wine and cheese than starters.

'Well, pretty soon you're into the whole argument of when does life begin, when is it viable, ensoulment etc.,' Gerry says. 'Which is both a complex biological and theological debate. But Ailish is right, David. Technically, they are both debates about self-determination.'

The main course is mercifully served and the conversation moves on. The wine is going down too fast now, but I'm calmer, and Gerry, comfortable here in his set, is clever and witty in a way I don't remember, an ally, a friend. He passes the potato gratin to me and smiles. If you'd asked me yesterday if I missed being part of a couple, I'd have said no. But today, yesterday feels lonely. And Gerry feels like home.

15

We start to date quietly, which Niall finds hilarious.

'Didn't you two go out together before? Why the secrecy? Is he an axe murderer? A child molester?' he says.

I swat him with a tea towel.

'Fuck off, you, and take out the bins. It's about all you're good for.'

'It's the relationship you're least likely to want to hide. He's straight – ish – seems like a nice guy, has money, a career with prospects, you have history – it couldn't be more fucking boring. Have you even told Fiona? *Uh*, imagine Barbara – she'll have a fucking *orgasm*.'

He swerves his bony frame out of my way, fake-ducking, before grabbing me from behind and tickling me.

'Get off me, I know where you've been. You perv.'

'We're here for a short time, might as well be a good time, baby. You know what I say – live fast, die young, leave a beautiful corpse.'

* * *

Niall won't tell anybody about Gerry until we're ready to go public, like I won't tell his secrets. Maybe that's what has drawn us together as friends, the unspoken. Even though I haven't told Niall about England, about Michael, if I did I know it would go no further, and he knows he can trust me too. Not that Niall is afraid to own his sexuality, be seen going into The George on a Friday night, to work behind the scenes for gay rights, but the fallout of a full declaration is something he's not ready for. Yet.

As for me, I've lain awake tortured nights, when Barbara is particularly bad maybe, wondering if I can trust him with my secret. When posters declaring *Thou Shalt Not Kill*, *Abortion Is Murder*, and images of bloody foetuses torture my head, march through my dreams, are my constant companions in the middle of the night. Concepts so ugly and awful I can't bear to share my reality of them with anybody. Not even Niall.

Gerry and I haven't told anybody we are – tentatively – back together, because this time we realise we need to be sure. Before involving other people, families, friends, making things complicated. I'm twenty-seven next year, too old to mess about in a relationship that is going nowhere if I want the conventional dream of children, a home, a husband. And, despite the antsy me who mocks these aspirations in others, I do. I am not Fiona. Somewhere in the confusion of my head is a picture of a kitchen, a table with children doing homework, a room filled with colour and aromas of baking and laughter. A place that is solid. Safe. Calling me.

We go on dates to the cinema, to dinner, the odd live music gig. Gerry's not much of a late-nighter, a dancer. We chat, we laugh, he stays over and we make love without pressure, the practised ease of two people used to each other's bodies. Pleasure points, foibles.

His eyes light with passion when he talks about his work. Literally following in the footsteps of his barrister father through the hallowed halls of educated justice. I accept that I will always be second priority if a client needs him, and I'm okay with that. If anything, I'm envious of his sense of purpose. As I trudge through the complex language of commercial contracts, advise on deals, I appreciate that while I like my job too and am good at it, there's also a bubbling resentment in me, an emptiness inherent in making or saving rich people money.

If – when – I think of Michael now it's less and more painful. Time and absence have dulled the longing, but in its place guilt and shame rankle. If it wasn't a great love, was I just a slut? I'll be somewhere random, in a queue in Tesco or on a bus maybe, and a wave of something like embarrassment will come over me. I will tear up. I'm not sure why or what for. A past that was. A future that might have been. A non-specific, but specific, loneliness that feels endless. An unfillable void.

I hear reports of my cousins through Barbara. They're doing well with the farm. Louisa and Ronan have two children. Joe and Helen are finally to marry. No babies for Sarah and Michael, she will say, with a glint I don't misinterpret. Somebody else walking her path. This particular grief. This longing. A pain which still lives in her. Sends her weekly to her doctor with another ailment, only for him to send her away with another prescription, which will comfort her, for a while.

Except when it doesn't.

Except when a pain lingers and a lump grows and she goes back to her doctor who realises with shock that, after all, it might not be her mind that's the problem.

'It's not looking good,' Frank says.

His face a mixture of sorrow, stupor and relief, the prospect of a life without Barbara a heady combination of terrifying and surely appealing. There are conversations with professionals he's not able for, his critical thinking impaired by emotion. I swoop, as if answering a calling from a higher entity, war declared, battle stations ready. As if I've been waiting for this, and this was inevitable. I arrange time off work, cancel a holiday, put Gerry on alert.

* * *

A cold-breath tiled room in St Vincent's hospital. Flecks of quartz glinting from solid terrazzo. Condensation hovering towards ice on ancient panes, climbing the steel rungs of a winter window towards a hopeful blue sky. A routine appointment with a Very Important Man in a white coat examining my mother, as I sit helpless, bear witness, no solace for her dignity stripped. He is thorough, his balding head arched to one side, nose hair tufting playfully into his moustache as his doughy white fingers, particularly trimmed nails, palpate breasts, underarms, shoulders. He motions to a student, a girl younger than I, to follow his lead. The communication between them is largely non-verbal, or maybe they are talking coherently but none of it makes sense through the buzzing interference in my brain. A raised eyebrow, a nod to Barbara's chart.

'Tumours in the right breast,' the girl says.

'Anywhere else?'

'No.'

'Are you sure?'

The girl flustered, embarrassed.

'I think so.'

'Look again.'

An apologetic half-glance, and she tries again, trounces the meat of my mother's shoulders searching for her prize. I will imagine later the room is completely airless. No breath when the girl nods to the Very Important Man and he nods back and they tell us, without telling us, without uttering a word, without the bare acknowledgment of our presence, that my mother's cancer has spread.

* * *

Life is consumed by the disease. The management of it, the dread of it, the excitement of it. Barbara starts to put her affairs in order. Initiating contact with people she hasn't seen in years to inform them of her imminent demise. Late-night chats with Brendan, with Elena. Grim justifications of doom over the garden wall with Kathleen Dunne, the everyday nature of disaster in our midst. Shock. Words. Emotion, absent.

There'll be time for that later.

Chemotherapy begins. I change my schedule to accommodate it. Ignore barely veiled threats at work about ruining my chances of promotion. I sit, when Frank can't or won't or simply isn't able, holding her hand as she sits in a high-backed chair, green pleather, poison wending its way through her veins. It might buy us time, which has morphed from an endless parade of days to our most precious commodity. When stilted conversation stalls, I go to the shop in the lobby, buy coffee, and we sift diligently through old *Hello* magazines as if searching for a cure. We flick past photos of lives we imagine we know, Lady Di's descent from grace, Julia Roberts on the red carpet, Amanda Holden marrying Les Dennis, almost old enough to be her father, a factoid irrelevant when dressed in raw silk and yellow roses.

'She looks so beautiful,' Barbara says.

The prospect of death has roused my mother from her slumber of despair. She'd long given up on hopes of a wedding, resigned herself to my 'damaged goods' status, envisaged a life for me as an 'old maid', perhaps eventually moving back home, looking after her and Frank. But. All the things-that-might-have-been weigh heavy now. Hope screaming its seduction only when somebody else has denied its existence.

'You would have made a beautiful bride,' she says.

The nearest thing to a compliment I can ever remember.

'I still might.'

'You might.'

And then, before I have thought through the consequences, simply wanting to extend the moment, to please her:

'Gerry and I are back together, Mum.'

16

The operation is scheduled for a Tuesday. I visit on Monday night with more grapes and a bottle of Lucozade, both of which she has taken a turn against, but there is little now that she hasn't. She semi-sits, pillows propped on smooth metal bars, which dig into the small of her back, sheathed only in slight pink cotton, hesitant skin. Purple rosary beads encrust her hands, fight for surface space with creeping worm-veins.

'*Hail Mary full of grace, the Lord is with thee ...*' she prays.

A mumble, as if it would be rude to articulate the words properly.

'*Our Father, who art in Heaven ...*'

'*Bless me, Father, for I have sinned ...*'

On repeat. Mantras. Penance. Payment for a debt that can never be met.

The woman is convinced she's going to Hell.

'The results are all good, Mum,' I say. 'There's every reason to hope that the operation will be successful.'

And there is. Chemotherapy has colluded with her body

chemistry and fought a good fight. The tumour is big, still six centimetres, but there is hope that it can be removed cleanly, the surrounding breast tissue excised as caution.

Hope, however, is not in Barbara's lexicon. Not anymore. A dirty word, a sentiment she's not entitled to. Something she sent on a plane to England long ago.

'I've left dinners in the fridge for the next two days, and there's chops and carrots for Thursday, Donegal Catch for Friday, with the small spuds and a few peas. You'll take him to McCormack's on Saturday?' she says.

'I will, Mum.'

'And Sunday you could ...'

Her voice trails. Too far ahead.

'I've written it all down for you. It's in the brown handbag on the shelf in the top of my wardrobe.'

I don't need to ask what 'it' is. And I probably don't need to even read the letter. She is to be waked at home. She is to be buried in her good purple dress, the one she wore at Christmas. Her coffin is to be made of oak, with panels and brass handles. One large arrangement of white lilies from the family, otherwise donations to St. Vincent de Paul. Details thrown in at side angles while we chat about *Coronation Street* or *Eastenders*. Details eating her head. Blowing mine.

Frank arrives and I escape St Anne's, ward of death, death chasing me down the lift shaft, the raised symbol on the button that calls it searing the skin of my forefinger, shooting aches through my body, wearying my flesh. Muscles that struggle to lift the burden of me. One foot in front of the other foot, through the wood-lined, clean-tiled, airy claustrophobia of the entrance vestibule, past the porter at the desk, who knows me now, nods to me, sympathy his default expression. Though likely the man is too saturated to feel it. To feel anything here, where fear and suffering are normalised, sanitised. Onwards, through the door, the side door, not the revolving door, which smacks somehow of misplaced frivolity, I join a stream of practically clad preoccupied people pouring into the dimlit evening. Brisk rather than cold. Haul prematurely ancient bones down the treelined shadows of Merrion Road, the paraphernalia of other lives popping visible through windows scattered on mansions, lined up in traffic. Imagine these lives. Imagine them carefree, caught in fixable woes: children's exam results, boardroom dramas, missed flights, what to choose from the menu at L'Ecrivain. Envy these lives.

* * *

When I arrive home, Gerry and Niall are in the kitchen. Niall is on a promise: a hint of blue eyeliner, a blue-green satin shirt, an air of intent. He puts his arm around me, squeezes me gently. Kisses the top of my head.

'Here she is,' he says. 'Aily McBailey. Tough day, my darling? I'm heading out on a date, but this lovely man here has just ordered pizza, so I know I'm leaving you in safe hands.'

'A Monday-night date? You were out all weekend.'

'Jaysis, my mother will never be dead while you're alive.'

The words form a current-situation-laden smog in the

warmth of low kitchen light. Gerry stifles a clearing of his throat.

'Your mother had a merciful release,' I say. 'If she could see the go-heck of you now. The poor woman must be spinning. Blue eyeliner? Does less is more mean nothing to you?'

Gerry doesn't get the dynamic between us, the nature of our slagging, the invisible safe-cushioned sides that mean we can say anything to each other and know it won't affect our foundations. Well. Almost anything.

When Niall leaves with a flourish, a flurry, Gerry takes me in his arms, the elongated squish-splash middle of him, fabric-softened Ralph Lauren shirt, tailored wool Louis Copeland suit, Hugo Boss aftershave. I curl in. Rub my nose, my forehead, lips, into the scent of him. Reach up to kiss him. Pull him to me. Every cell of my body desperate for obliteration. Feel him respond. Feel him pull back. He takes my head in his hands and kisses the top of it.

'I picked up a couple of *Friends* videos on the way over,' he says. 'Go get changed, you're exhausted.'

He shoos me to my room, pulls on a jumper he has left folded on a chair, deliberately, probably, for school-night spontaneity.

I put my pyjamas on. Run a cotton ball with cleanser across my cheeks, my eyes, catch remnants of make-up undisturbed by tears. Slowly rub moisturiser into the contours of the face in the mirror, which is pale, exhausted. Lips a line. Cheeks round from months now of eating on the hoof between work and hospital appointments. Pizza holds no appeal. My breasts and thighs strain checked brushed cotton. I'm a mess. Another tear slides down my nose.

I grab my blanket from the end of my bed, take it to the sitting room, where pizza has arrived, is splayed in cardboard on the coffee table, napkins, plates, a bottle of red, two glasses, a box of hankies. A hot water bottle, and the length of Gerry, open and ready to cuddle me.

'We can talk about it? Or not, whatever you prefer. No pressure,' he says.

'I'm so tired.'

'How is she?'

'Terrified.'

'It must be ...'

'Yep, it must be. Whatever.'

He pulls me close, smoky pub smells from his jumper, a comfort.

'I love you,' he says.

He has said this before. He's said it a lot recently. We say it, always, when we make love. A prayer to justify the animal act.

'I wouldn't be able to get through this without you,' I say.

And it's true. He has been there, every step, a stalwart. Phoning or calling around most evenings, always taking my calls in the office, even if he is working on something consuming, even if, possibly, it might incur the wrath of his father. He holds me now, a little tighter. A hint of stubble on my shiny forehead, my greasy hair melding into his collar. Another tear escaping. A wave of emotion between us, an energy, me in a heady space beyond exhaustion, finding an anchor.

'You don't have to get through anything without me, Ail,' he says. 'I know this is shit timing, and I will ask you properly, I promise, but I want to be here for you through all the things, good and bad. You mean everything to me. And you don't have to answer or think of this now, but I want to marry you.'

The tears come now in force, and I'm not sure if it's gratitude, or grief, for the girl who sat on a sofa eleven years ago with her cousin's now husband, in her cousin's robe, trying on her cousin's life, if it's the death of her, or the birth of me, the expunging of sin, a redirection of pain from all the years of yearning, transformation into hope, joy, and yes, love. The promise of home, a grateful skidding arrival at fourth base. I will never truly know which ingredient of this cocktail drives me in the moment.

'Yes,' I say. 'If and when you ask, the answer is yes.'

'How old were you when you married?'

'Twenty-six. Nearly twenty-seven.'

'Young.'

'By today's standards. Too young, maybe.'

'Has it been a good marriage?'

'Define good,' you say.

'That's different for everybody.'

You look to the floor. To the door.

'Gerry is a good husband. I mean, he's tried.'

Breathe.

'I haven't always been a great wife.'

17

I feel like Lady Di with her face already on the memorabilia: mugs, tea towels, key rings, her – my – fate set. The everyday consumed with dress fittings and floral arrangements and seating plans. A winter wedding, timing accelerated to accommodate the ever-present potential for Barbara's health to deteriorate. She's doing well. The operation was a success. Her hair is growing back, fuzzy and strange and she will need to wear a wig for the Big Day. But. New Life where none was expected. Fertility on barren ground. A miracle.

Frank floats with what can only be the demeanour of a man who had been facing a Green Mile walk granted an unforeseen reprieve with an unquantified time limit. Stunned. Still despairing. Ever hopeful.

'It's an answer to all our prayers ...' he says.

'Borrowed time ...' he says.

'Isn't it great what they can do nowadays, all the same, modern science ...' he says.

Conspiratorial whispers. Hopeless exhalations. He's still only sixty-two. Has been to the brink and back, all the complications of Barbara. He will go on. Welded to her now. But he could conceivably start again. Suck some joy out of the time he has left, running like sand through an egg-timer on speed. Find another Auntie Elena. Find this one, who arrives on a cloud of Chanel with the heft of Louisa in tow and her two toddling cute daughters, whom I've asked to be my flower girls.

'Oh, Ailish, so lovely,' Elena says. 'You will be such a beautiful bride, just like Sarah. I think they look a little alike don't you, Frank? I know the colouring is different, but they both have Granny Carmel's cheekbones, the eye shape, the lips. Beautiful girls.'

Louisa watches her mother. Her body settled resolutely now into a series of squares, face weary with her own motherhood. I feel for her. She doesn't get the acknowledgement even of having been a beautiful bride, a day when surely even the plainest girl can claim divine intervention, fairy dust to single her out.

Elena is so caught in the trials and tribulations of beautiful Sarah, she can't recognise the look of pain and resignation on her second daughter's face.

'Seeing a daughter married means so much to a mother, Ailish,' she says. 'Especially poor Barbara. After all she's been through.'

As always, Elena sends me to multiple places simultaneously. An energy which is warm yet threatening, powerful in its potential either way. The mention of her name is enough to make me wary. I want to hate her for the hold I perceive she has over my father. But I love her, for her kindnesses. And now I'm older, sometimes, I can forgive her blind spots, excuse them as human frailty. She's ageing badly. Marionette lines cut deep cheek to chin, her flesh thin and crepey, mottled from too much sun, not enough sunscreen. I can see she's right about Sarah looking like Granny now, her lines cut clearer, an Irish hunger, which does, in fact, resemble my own face. The thought pleases me. That Sarah and I are similar. That I may have some claim on her mystique.

And I know I want this because no matter all that has happened since, a part of my head is, might always be, anchored in that dusty little sitting room in Portobello, when for a few moments I was Sarah. I inhabited her. I borrowed her life. Every moment clear, every detail set – the dirty patch of raw wood where whoever varnished the stairs missed a bit, the tarnished brass rings on the sash windows, the fuzzy yellow street light dancing through the fringe on the shade on the standard lamp. The delicious feeling of skin-on-skin for the first time. Unrepeatable. Unforgiveable. Unimaginable now.

* * *

Barbara and I go shopping for a dress that will hide and display her. High collars are preferred but hard to find, the plunging Vs and cami tops in vogue too exposing. We settle on a turquoise blue mid-length, pleated skirt, a crewneck style, the colour so vibrant and unexpected it pulls her eyes from their sockets. With matching hat, neatly cut ash-blonde wig and new pink lipstick she looks like a different human. The effect on Frank is startling, as if he's seeing a ghost. More than the visual changes, there's a muted euphoria to her which I suspect has as much to with do her medication as the excitement of the wedding.

Wedding excitement too, though, is muted. There is only so much that can be managed. I clean the house and buy in food for random guests, organise an awkward tea and sandwiches pre-wedding catch-up with Gerry's parents, wheel in Brendan and Elena. The intention of their presence is tribal support, but the effect is laborious. Our house is too small and too swathed in sickness to house them, so they stay the week before the wedding in the Rochestown Lodge Hotel, head to Dublin on day trips, take Frank to the pub, deposit his maudlin carcass back with me, a prisoner now in my childhood bedroom, minding everybody, missing Niall, and the flat, and the freedom of Merrion Square. Some essential part of me, some important essence, forever now unrealised, hovering in watchful breaths amidst the crack and pile of that place, a dissipating mist on the bedsheets.

Gerry's mother is less than pleased with my reappearance. Moira is far too well-bred to admit a twitch of this, but it's there in the small tics of judgement those of her ilk make when mingling with lesser mortals.

'Isn't it wonderful that you have all this country heritage, Ailish? I didn't realise your mother was quite so *rural*. It must have been a huge adjustment for her coming to Dublin when she was what ...?'

'Seventeen.'

'Seventeen? Just after her Leaving Certificate?'

I nod. Confirm the qualification.

'To go to college?'

'To go to Dublin Castle, the Civil Service.'

I picture Barbara, packed carefully up to Dublin by well-meaning and proud Granny Carmel, all sensible shoes and knickers and doing the right thing only to be found wanting here, at the pinnacle of her ambition, years of practised accent blown to bits in the sharply honed spotlight of Moira's trained eye.

I give my mother a self-conscious hug. Random acts of affection are more commonplace between us now. We sit and watch television and plan my big day and occasionally I might pat her on the shoulder, try to squeeze her hand. She brushes me off, but not enthusiastically, almost reluctantly, as if to say she is fine, really, and we look again at swatches of material for Fiona's bridesmaid dress together, sashes for the flower girls. Table decorations. Music for the service and the band. Plans she is able for.

'You're not okay,' Fiona says.

'I'm fine.'

'You shouldn't be rushing into this.'

'I'm not rushing into anything. I've known Gerry forever.'

'You're in an emotionally heightened state. A form of grief. This is a huge decision. You shouldn't make it under pressure. Put it off, Ailish. If only for a few months.'

'I can't.'

'Why not?'

I can't answer. Though I can. I can tell her time is the problem. Mum may not have long, I can make her last while happy, that she is happy, that finally there is peace between us. A restitution. I can tell her this.

But Fiona already knows.

Some of it.

Gerry, on the other hand, seems unaware of pressure. We're seeing less of each other since Mum left the hospital, since I've been spending time at home. The days are flying into weeks and the wedding is fast approaching. When we snatch moments together, he is distracted, a big case, but it should be finished in time for us to go on our honeymoon to Portugal. We'll spend time together then. But maybe just one week. His father has another client in the offing, dates to be set, and it could all happen quite quickly. High profile, big money. It will be worth it.

More guests arrive and take residence with Frank in the bar. I wonder that I didn't notice before how much he drinks these days. How it skipped my radar. Now that he's taken a few days off work, I can see it, the want hitting in around lunchtime, a steady pace throughout the day. Not enough to get visibly drunk or obstreperous. Enough to simply take the edge off.

Sarah and Michael, Joe and Helen join the others the day before the wedding. Joe and Helen have left their five-month-old baby, Eoin, at home, a source of some distress to Helen, who is not finished weaning him, but Elena is adamant that the presence of a baby might upset Sarah.

Sarah has had another miscarriage. Sarah has had three miscarriages we know of, maybe more. She looks gaunt, haunted, a look that is currently in and selfishly makes me more aware of the couple of extra hospital-visiting pounds around my thighs which are proving hard to shift. She's brought me a gift. A wedding-planning album, a tacky-looking thing, white and pink, hearts and bows. So incongruent with my perception of her, it takes a minute to process.

'Sorry, I know it's probably a bit late,' she says. 'But you can still fill it with all the plans. I pressed a couple of flowers from my bouquet into mine, put in swatches in from my dress and Louisa's. All the photos, obviously.'

I flick through it and see there is a page with a basic family tree. An allowance for offspring.

'It's lovely.'

I press her hand. See the tiredness in her. The sadness in her. She'd been working as a student counsellor in Carlow IT, but she hasn't worked this past two years, maybe more, not since the first miscarriage, at twenty weeks. She likely has the top tier of her wedding cake carefully stowed in a box in her huge utility room, the house they built at the far end of the farm, bordering Michael's parent's land, a mansion intended for a big family. No doubt a nursery decorated and waiting.

Michael looks tired too. Disappointed. In life. In love? I catch him, during dinner, during drinks, looking at me. A look that is infuriating in its specificity. Rests too long for comfort. Smacks of ... interest? Longing?

Maybe I'm imagining that.

But.

Maybe not.

'You look great,' he says.

Me: by the sink, pulling plates, sorting sandwiches, side-angled, side-eyed.

'You really do,' he says. 'You look lovely.'

Lovely.

And he's sheepish, in a floppy, deliberately endearing sort of way. Apologising without apologising? A boychild who accidentally broke a window, smashed the car up, killed the dog?

I want to smack him.

I want to forgive him.

I want to smack him.

I continue with the clean-up. Hand him a plate. Avoid his eyes. Shrug. Which might be a forgiveness. Is certainly not a smack. Actively avoid him for the duration. And the more I do this, the more he seems present. Everybody's friend. Quietly attentive, buying pints, helping with chores. I record every image, etch every movement in the part of my brain commonly mistaken for a heart. And I know this is pure self-torture, self-loathing, but I could easier stop breathing.

'Such a nice young man,' Barbara says.

And everyone agrees.

* * *

We have a family dinner in the hotel the night before the wedding. I wear a long red skirt and a black T-shirt with sequins, strappy sandals, fresh hair. Far more glamorous than my usual look.

'Bit late to be looking for an alternative now,' Fiona says.

'Don't be stupid.'

'You're not sure. It's written all over you.'

And she's right. I'm not sure of anything. But I'm on a path. Faces – Mum, Frank, Elena, Brendan, Fiona, Gerry, Louisa, Ronan, Joe, Helen, Sarah, Michael … everywhere I look, expectation. I smile, affect the right emotions. Time slips into slow mode. I'm hyperaware of everybody at the table, all the plays, all the shapes and patterns of relationships, the history. The faces they are putting on. All of us. Masks.

'Gerry isn't second best,' you say.

A different day, a different light through the window, a different you.

'You sound like you've been thinking about that,' the woman says.

'I have.'

'Have you reached any conclusions?'

'I would have argued, up to now, that Gerry has never really seen me.'

'And now?'

'Maybe I've never taken the time to properly see him.'

Breathe. Sip. Breathe.

'I mean, I've spent a large part of our marriage thinking about somebody else.'

18

February 2006

I stand, taut, in a landscape of cupboard carcasses and concrete dust, on the cusp of explosion. Implosion. A fine grey talc coating me, my trainers, tracksuit, hands, hair, nails, invading my nostrils, ears, head, all pounding with the excited chatter of seven-year-olds.

'We don't want bunk beds again, Mummy – there's five bedrooms now, can we not have our own rooms?' Saoirse says.

'But we can't afford new beds, Mummy said, didn't you, Mummy? We're already *over budget*,' Róisín says.

'But the beds pull apart, don't they, Mummy? We can have one each in our own rooms. Tell her, Mummy. Tell her we can have our own rooms. The house is so much bigger now, isn't it, Mummy? Mummy?'

'*Shush*, girls, *shush*. I can't hear myself think.'

I imagine me in the aftermath of a spontaneous combustion, images from the real-life-story trash mags of my teens, bloody leg stubs protruding from sensible boots. Consider the kitchen island intently, grip the black marble worktop, push finger and thumb-pads hard onto the slick cold of it. Clench my teeth. Gold mica chips pinging before my eyes.

Róisín, always the more sensitive twin, puts her hand on my thigh, and I jump.

'Jesus, Róisín, can you not just give me a second.'

Tears tickle my nose. Irritate The Persistent Guilt. I'm not the mother I want to be. The kind of mother I think I would have wanted. All floral serenity and apple pie on one hand, laptop and feminist torch in the other.

An ideal. An aspiration. An impossibility.

'I love you, Mummy,' Róisín says.

An accusation.

* * *

My pregnancy with the twins was riven with anxiety. I think of it even now and I shudder. The guilt that forbade me enjoy it. The plundered memory of a maybe Faustian pact, made when out of my mind and feral the first time I fell: let me not be pregnant and I will forever renounce my right to motherhood. Something like that. A blessing undeserved. The forerunner to fulfilment of a curse. Those early days a blur of sore breasts and runaway body, the shell of me sundered, delight blunted, and then revelled in, glorious sweet gasps of right, competence, purpose. Magic. The fear of bad karma. Fluctuating notions of justice. The wild swings.

The girls were born in a rush of good hormones which floundered quickly on a shore of judgement. My own. Double wondrous luck, Saoirse arriving exactly fifteen minutes after Róisín, identical, elfin creatures, translucent and fragile, almost too beautiful and otherworldly to exist in this one. They terrified me. Delicate fingers stretching in glassy fronds from tiny metacarpals. Other babies were unformed chubby things. Mine were born elegant. Camera ready. From the first day they knew how to strike a pose, Gerry click-click-clicking his Nikon. I smiled too. The girls completed us.

On days when I was exhausted, I powered through. Allowed myself no weakness. Juggled moments of awe with shit and sore breasts, the horror of colic and mastitis, the exquisite persistent torture of watching them sleep. The fear I might sleep through one of them breathing their last. The weight of responsibility which landed on my chest at 3 am threatened suffocation. My attention to them was absolute. No minor detail unnoticed, no small joy undocumented, no real or imagined threat unthwarted. Nothing mattered more than these fairy children.

Before their second birthday I crashed. Mother interventions, GP visits. A short course of pills. Not post-natal depression, they said, not even proper depression. A mild case of burn-out, Moira diagnosed, nothing serious.

'You just need to push through, Ailish,' my mother said. 'Motherhood is hard work.'

I couldn't resolve for her the material differences of our experience. My luck in not having to wash and dry nappies, a car under my arse, salaries which afforded childcare. My two-for-one deal which granted me the luxury of a ready-made family, the 'only child' pressure and stigma thwarted up front.

Couldn't reconcile or explain the difference and sameness of our despair.

* * *

'Maybe you need to try the Lexapro again?' Gerry says now. 'You only needed it for a short time last time. It's not addictive or anything.'

'Maybe I need to not be working full-time with twins and a monstrosity of a house extension going pear-shaped?' I say. 'And you disappearing off God-knows-where four days a week?'

'I have to work, love,' he says.

As if he is sanity and stability itself.

And I am fundamentally unreasonable.

'When Lakeview is finished we can look at you going part-time, maybe even taking some time off completely to be with the girls.'

But they're already in first class, and time is slipping by so fast, and the busyness is unbearable. When I imagine the shape and form of my life it looks like a series of primary-coloured paper boxes – arts-and-craft cut-outs – overflowing with random paraphernalia, fixtures and fittings, official-looking documents, pots and pans and teddy bears, tenuously held together with paperclips and elastic bands. The entire construction wobbling dangerously, threatening to overflow. To spill.

* * *

Some of the mums from school have formed a book club and invited me to join. I'm a hit-and-miss reader, I don't have the time, but I'm assured the only skill required is to be able to drink wine, and this I can do with aplomb. The thought of a Friday-night glass pulls me through the week, a normal week, but since we moved to a cramped rental to facilitate the builders and the extension, I feel a Thursday glass is justified, Wednesday is optional, and sure who is going to judge a woman for oiling a lonely Tuesday night watching *Desperate Housewives* with a sip or two of Pinot Grigio? Once the children have completed their homework with a sufficient display of effort, are nutritiously fed and safely tucked up in bed, sure where's the harm?

I've never been much of a joiner, but the book-clubbers are a homogenous group. All eight of us, though varying mildly in shape and hair-colour and size, look a lot like me. We wear Tommy Hilfiger jeans and Carl Scarpa boots, preppy Ralph Lauren jumpers. Our children go to the same private schools, our husbands are employed in solid professions: barristers, solicitors, bankers, accountants, one dentist. We holiday three or four times a year, ski and sun sojourns mandatory, romantic mini-breaks to keep our marriages kicking. There's a slow-burn undercurrent of sniffiness when we talk about Elaine, who didn't go to university, is married to a builder. They've bought a three-storey on Ulverton Road in Dalkey and are in the middle of effusive and extensive renovations, marble bathrooms, gold taps and suchlike. A bit tacky, is the consensus. But Mary, married to banker Jim, our natural leader and a doctor in her own right if you can count a PhD, is all over her, vocally supportive of the small fortune they're pouring into restoring original features because, after all, property is a solid investment. Second homes all the rage. House prices have risen three hundred percent in the past ten years. The banks are encouraging it, doling out mortgages like lottery tickets. Even our cleaners are buying in Bulgaria.

Yet. Amidst all this clamour and chatter, I'm reluctant to mention Lakeview.

* * *

Moira can't reconcile our house 'choice' with the future she imagined for her only son.

'Don't mind her,' Gerry says. 'You know how she is — anything not double-fronted Georgian is a council house in her world. The house is grand. For all the reasons you say – it's near schools, transport, your friends. Big garden, potential to extend again if we want. It's grand.'

We've come late to the property market, after prices started soaring. Getting legal careers started takes time, Gerry's income is hit and miss, dependent on his client base, dependent on his contacts, and only a few short years ago, the banks were fussy about such things. The house is grand. Detached. A 1970s bungalow in a convenient location for buses. The periphery of Killiney. The guts of a million euro and God knows how much more now before this extension is completed. When his mother visits, I flicker between holding an argumentative tongue and trying not to apologise, for surely such a travesty has something to do with my lack-of-original-features pedigree. I take sugar-coated barbs about modern fireplaces and eyebrows that decry the deep vulgarity of our American-style-fridge-on-order and offer them up in penance. She has a nice relationship with the girls. Takes them to the cinema and shopping once or twice a month, time I am grateful for.

Time I spend with Barbara, who is also nervous about the extension. I'm careful mentioning sums of money to her. Too many zeros can induce a tailspin. I'll only be home from dropping her off when I'll have Frank on the phone, stressing her fragility, the persistently precarious state of her health. Though the woman, apart from normal wear and tear, is as healthy as the proverbial horse now. Since the cancer, she minds herself fastidiously. For once in her life, approaching seventy, she has a cushion of meat on her bones and, while she still looks somewhat vaporous, you can give her a hug without fear of doing damage. Not that she likes hugs any more than she used to. If I give her one, I realise it's more for my benefit, for the benefit of the girls, who are all about the hugs at the moment, and I don't need a psychology degree to tell me I'm trying to normalise a standard of physical affection across generations.

As if it was always a given.

Something I too received and deserved.

Receive and deserve.

Though not so much from Gerry. Not at the moment. You know how these things go through phases. They talk about it in the book club, joke about their sex lives. A glass or two too many and some give more detail than required. No matter how many glasses I have, this is not something I like to, want to, can talk about. Some things are private. And from what I gather, fallow periods are normal in long-term relationships. Not a cause for concern. Besides, apart from all the other demands on his time, on his headspace, Gerry now has the road to Tullamore worn into the DNA of the tyres of his BMW, checking up on and into the progress of Lakeview.

Lakeview. If the zeros involved in renovating a dormer bungalow in South County Dublin give Barbara palpitations, a glimpse at the accounts for Lakeview would finish her. They haunt me at night, Gerry snoring gently, deeper, rising to a crescendo, until I poke him in the ribs with an elbow, or kick a heel at his bum, resentful of his rest. Though I know he's worried about it too, the overruns. The questionable competence of Ronan. Louisa's husband is forty now and balding, driving two Mercedes, a saloon for business and a two-seater soft top for weekend fun with Louisa and the girls. Trips to Adare Manor, Mount Juliet. The K-Club for Sunday lunch.

* * *

It started in the K-Club. A year and a half ago, nearly two, at the christening of Ciarán, finally arrived offspring of Sarah and Michael. A massive and deserved celebration, Sarah radiant in Versace, Michael all proud pink cheeks and buy-you-another-drink. I'm happy for them, but it's a happiness tinged somehow, a bitterness I can almost taste, copper-like on my tongue, floating in me, with me, as I move amongst tables laden with linen and sparkle, half-full glasses, aperitifs, wine for different courses. Gerry and I, enmeshed on the second family table with Ronan and Louisa, Joe and Helen, Frank and Barbara. Me, worried about the girls, staying overnight with Moira.

'They'll be grand,' Gerry says. 'For God's sake, it's okay to let your hair down every now and then, Ailish. You don't have to be glued to them twenty-four-seven to prove you're a Good Mother.'

I'm obsessed with being a Good Mother, he tells me. And I am. Have a library of books on the subject, as if it is something I can learn, improve upon, as I regard my mother now, across the table, gin and orange in her hand, a look of faint bemusement, oblivious to half the goings-on around her. To Ronan and Joe enticing Gerry to the gents, to the cut and lift of them upon their return, the chatter which has risen an octave or two, careering towards bravado, and it strikes me, forcibly, that though we live in physical proximity, Barbara and I inhabit entirely different worlds.

Maybe we all do.

'It's a sure-fire thing,' Ronan says.

'I'm still raging I missed the opportunity to buy a house here,' Joe says.

'We have the membership,' Helen says 'The boys can still play golf at the weekends.'

'This is business we're talking about, Helen,' Ronan says. 'Investment. I know a couple of lads on the council – there'd be no problem getting the land rezoned. Just had a chat there with Michael's father. If he gives Michael the bottom field we have access. Brendan is on board for giving over the top field. He's no use for it anyway, now he's cut back the herd. Elena wants to spend more time at their place in Spain.'

'It's a no-brainer, Gerry,' Joe says. 'And it'd be great to have a solicitor on board.'

'I'm a barrister. Criminal law's more my thing,' Gerry says.

'Even better.'

They guffaw. In unison.

'How does Michael feel about it?' Gerry says.

'Michael's in. He doesn't have money to invest, the land from his da would be his input. The land from Brendan, Joe's. We'd need to raise capital from the banks. But that's my area of expertise. I know the mortgage guys from AIB in the town well, Bank of Ireland too, if needs be. They're always helping clients of mine get houses over the line, few tickets for the rugby, a day or two out here or there, they're pals. A solicitor – a *barrister* – as part of the consortium would be icing on the cake for them. Look good for head office.'

'I don't have to invest?'

'Well, not actual cash. You'd have to sign the loan documents. Put your house up as collateral probably, but it's a sure thing. Safe as houses.'

More laughter.

Clink-clink-fizz.

'We reckon we'll get planning for at least a hundred and fifty,' Joe says. 'Even if we sell them for two hundred grand a piece, that's thirty mil. Minus costs.'

'Who's going to buy them?' I say.

They'd forgotten I was there. Look at me as if I'm a newly landed alien.

'How do you mean?' Ronan says.

'What I just said. Who are you going to sell to?'

'Commuters. Dubliners. They can't get out of the place quick enough, better quality of life in the country. Sure all round here is riddled with them.'

He waves an unsteady hand. I presume he means Kildare. All three of them look at me. Six eyes aglaze. Pupils dilated. Joe's mocking and sly, Ronan's buried small in his plate face, Gerry's laden with innate confidence in his own opinion, politely feigning openness, waiting for an argument to be put forth so he can demonstrate the systematic validity of his own. And I wonder if it is me who is the problem, if I am the weakest link here, if it is my conservative peasant blood or the inherent fears of motherhood which make me see risk where others see opportunity. A deficiency of class or gender. Maybe both.

'But, lads, this is deepest darkest Tullamore we're talking about,' I say. 'Offaly, not the Riviera. You're five miles out from town. Where are the facilities? The roads, the schools, the pubs, restaurants and coffee shops? The infrastructure?'

'It's just over an hour from Dublin,' Ronan says. 'You'd be longer getting the DART from Bray into town. And people don't think that way anymore, Ailish. They want quality of life with their families, better built homes, fresh air. The coffee shops and restaurants will come. Tullamore is on the up. We're not country hicks anymore.'

'Yeah, cuz,' Joe says. 'We've gone all cosmopolitan when you weren't looking.'

19

Strictly speaking, the Volvo is mine, but Gerry insists on driving longer journeys, insists on driving any time we are in a car together, unless he is pissed after a match or a function and I'm picking him up from Lansdowne Road, some random pub or nightclub in town.

'It's wurk,' he'll say. 'Netwurking.'

A beery belch permeating the soft cream-leather interior.

When I am in the mood to be receptive to it, there's something endearing about Gerry in these moments. Cute. A vulnerability he doesn't often show, and it's not that I like him better when he's drunk, but he relaxes, softens in a way that makes me realise how much stress he usually carries in him. Stress that expensive gym and golf club memberships do nothing to alleviate. Mostly because he doesn't go.

'I don't have the time,' he says. 'Between work and the kids, sure the weekends are taken up with all the activities and birthday parties.'

And so we bow to peer pressure, try out the latest greatest accessory.

The *Au Pair*.

All the rage with my book clubbers.

'Sofia is just so *maternal*,' Mary says. 'The boys adore her. Though she has me eaten out of house and home. Well, she's a big girl.'

We titter, envious of this perfect combination. A cost-effective young one who can take your place at bath and story time, babysit, feed your children and not threaten your marriage.

'You hear such stories.'

And you do. It's a risk, bringing nubile Mediterranean skin into your home, under the watchful eye of your oh-so-faithful-husband, just at the tipping point where you yourself may be starting to wilt, weary with worry and wine. And you can't actually demand an ugly one. It's not politically correct.

Genevieve's pictures are ambiguous. In one, where the light is poor, she looks blurry pretty. In another, better light, she is wearing spectacles, which give her a rather stern air. She's a teacher from Marseilles, twenty-six, older than most, wanting to improve her English for the summer, and to be honest, I'm so worn by this point, if Pamela Anderson landed in her best *Baywatch* bikini willing to take on the lot of them — Gerry included, maybe especially — I reckon I'd be happy to leave her to it.

The reality in the rear-view mirror now is disconcerting. The girl has, in spades, what all women really want – style. A quirky head-tilt, an endearing habit of half-shrugging tanned shoulders, an aura of amusement. A sudden laugh. Magic and sparkle. I sit up front, apply liberal Rouge Velvet Allure to dehydrated colourless lips, whilst she perches prettily between my entranced daughters, murdering '*Frère Jacques*'.

'*Dormez vous? Dormez vous?*' Gerry chirps.

I sideswipe him a 'Really?' look, and he grins.

'Loosen up, Ail. We're going on our holibops.'

I will never regard Tullamore as a holiday destination. The familiar cut of hedgerow, the pervasive bovine undercurrent, induce a bilious response, churned and heightened by the beautiful day, an electrical fault which is maintaining the leather passenger seat heat on a constant low setting. A slick of sweat forms on my inner thighs, threatens a trickle, a stain on my silky Monsoon skirt.

'This car needs a service,' I say.

'It's on the spreadsheet,' he says. 'Next month.'

I know this. I'm intimate with the spreadsheet. Its rigid lines, vagaries and immutabilities. Leinster season tickets and foreign holidays awarded equal billing with mortgage and school fees, as we charge groceries to credit cards building up a steam, a habit I sense is an undiscussed norm in the book club, talk of informal loans to and from family, allowance for our own adolescent attitudes towards gratification whilst we rigorously limit our children's screen time. I'm not unaware. Most of us aren't. But the spending has reached fever pitch and *need* is subjective. Reality can be subverted, distracted by baubles. We're living our best lives.

* * *

We stop at the electric gates, the legend *Mannion Estate* in cursive wrought-iron script across an archway that is just high enough for trucks, a monstrosity à la South Fork, an etching of which appears now as the logo on produce from the farm shop. The necessity to get out of the car to press the buzzer and request access irritates me in a way the physical opening and closing of gates for cattle safety never did. I curse silently as the stiletto heel of my sandal catches in the grating.

I've made an effort. Got my hair coloured and cut. A strappy white T-shirt and a spray tan. I always do, coming here, try to look my best, hold my own, as if I am a bona fide option beside Sarah. Beside Genevieve now. A tenuous forage for my femininity. In reality, I'm so exhausted I don't think any man would consider me as an option for anything. It's only so I can stand tall in my own head, cast another me in some fantasy romcom where I'm the one who got away, I'm the one who is obsessed over, a script where Michael regrets every day that he didn't choose me. Anything to distract from the lonely dull ache of longing which catches still when I'm low. A yearning for something, something other, and I'm no longer naïve enough to think that's necessarily Michael.

Michael. The man hovers on the outskirts of these gatherings, caught up in watchful fatherhood, in the flow of his own latest enterprise, this time a petting farm, which runs alongside the shop and bakery, the almost-laid-foundations for a café. Expansions which produce chronic bouts of cognitive dissonance in my mother, who can't reconcile her puritanical upbringing with such colourful excess. Veers wildly between predicting an inevitable divine retribution and boasting to the neighbours.

'Your granny wouldn't recognise the place if she came back now,' she says.

And she wouldn't. I struggle to recognise it myself, it changes so vastly from one visit to the next.

The girls pile from the car, excited to see their cousins, unleash their own constrained wild into the rough and tumble of Joe's boys. Curly-headed Daniel, a year and a bit older, making his Communion tomorrow, is why we are here. One of the reasons.

Louisa's girls, teenagers now, scoop my two up, delighted to have pretty playthings, fascinated, as most are, with my daughters almost perfect duplication. Externally, at least.

We land in the kitchen, stainless steel and cool lines and fancy gadgets, a place I can't find Granny Carmel at all, except to imagine her in a corner in apparition form, blessing herself in wonder at the sight.

Genevieve, blithe blemishless legs in a flirty skirt that covers none of them, gravitates towards Elena who, as usual, is conducting us.

Elena has taken up baking at an almost professional level, her creations more fine art than culinary delight, though that too. They're lodging on her hips, her former sway a shuffle, the pain of osteoarthritis etched in skin loose and lined in generous jowls. She places, with self-conscious care, a delicate selection of pink-white-yellow cupcakes on a tiered Wedgwood cake stand resplendent with peonies. Coos softly at my wide-eyed, sugar-hungry offspring, bids them admire her work. The decimation of her beauty moves me temporarily back in time, to her youth, the old kitchen, child-me at the table, an insider, yet an outsider. Sparks a tear for all the change. Maybe. I brush it away quickly.

Sarah is sitting sunlit by the window which is a wall which frames the landscape beyond, a horizon of mute florals and vibrant greens, broken by the occasional well-placed cow. A fancy stove, new since last visit, is lit, despite the summer's day, despite the folding doors, an outside-in aspiration better suited to a different climate. Curled, on the squishy leather sofa, tight to his mother's breast, is Ciarán, two and a bit, coddled and shy. A huge suspicious eye on him, a heartbreakingly dimpled hand clasping his milky sustenance as if his life still depended upon it. He is all his father, golden in his mother's skin.

I make a face at him, smile, sidle up, try to engage, reach a hand out to tickle, caress his foot, but he shrugs away my bait, whimpers.

'No worries, little man,' I say. And to Sarah: 'How are things?'

'Okay,' she says. 'You know yourself.'

But I don't. And I do. Yet I don't.

She's had another miscarriage. Unspoken grief upon grief. So many now, the occurrence is almost commonplace. Some maybe no more than a delayed period, that oh-so-everyday confirmation of expectation. So many, nobody is counting any more. Nobody, except Sarah. The resonant sorrow is writ deep on her face in the heightened wonder with which she regards her child who lives.

'Mama says he's too big to nurse now,' she says. 'But it comforts him.'

'Well, keep going then. Comfort is no small thing.'

I pat her hand with affection. Affection that is felt, deep. The loss of a child is no small thing.

'Barbara's not coming down for the Communion?' Sarah says.

'She's poorly, the knee is acting up, and she's acting the martyr,' I say. 'Frank says it wouldn't be worth it.'

We grimace. Then smile. A shared knowing.

'Hey, Little Man,' Michael says.

Appearing on the granite-slabbed patio, backlit in an orange-pink late-May heat tease. I hold myself imperceptibly straighter. Ciarán squirms tighter to his mother's flesh, moans, a soft rhythmic bleat.

'Hey, Ailish.'

'Hey.'

'Did Dan Burke arrive with the coffee machines?' Sarah says.

'Yeah. There's something wrong with the second one, though, an electrical fault. He's bringing it back to see if they can fix it.'

'It's brand new, shouldn't have any faults. Is he sending it to the manufacturer or trying to sort it himself?'

'I didn't ask.'

'Well, do. They cost a fortune, too much for Dan Burke to be tinkering with in his back room.'

'I thought the foundations were only going down for the coffee shop?' I say.

'They are,' Michael says. 'But it's the petting zoo – the parents want their mochas and cappuccinos and lattes, what have ye. We're going to put a couple of machines in the bakery till we're set. All the margin is in coffee anyway.'

'It's all go. Michael's pure exhausted in the evenings, we hardly see him. If he's not mucking out the pens or feeding animals he's at the computer half the night with the spreadsheets.'

'Has to be done. Got to give you the best start, don't we, fella?'

He moves to ruffle Ciarán's hair. The child pulls away again, Sarah snuggles him closer and, maybe I'm only fancying it, but my formerly hopeful eye might detect a frost between the happy couple. Not that I'd truly wish or want that now. Life is complicated enough.

* * *

The sugar is kicking in, dialling up the noise level, children crawling from every inconvenient nook. Ronan and Joe arrive from the bowels of the ever-expanding farmhouse. There's something wolverine about these two together, something to do with Joe's sharp angles, Ronan's stretched gut. They walk as if to a beat. Spot Genevieve at precisely the same time.

'Well, hello, who's this?' Ronan says.

Lips wet with saliva, hips splayed, grandeur and swagger.

Genevieve is unfazed. The girl is used to this. She's busying putting out plates, moving effortlessly from sink to fridge, filling the kettle. A symphony in physical form. Michael looks at her too, I notice. And Sarah notices. And the room fills, as if with an invisible, odourless vapour. Hormones and possibility and danger. The sudden scent of sex.

20

The girls are keen to see the pig. All the animals but, particularly, the pig. Maisie.

'They should have called her Peppa,' Róisín says.

'Peppa is a stupid name,' Saoirse says.

'Saoirse is a stupid name.'

'You're stupid.'

'No, I'm not.'

'Yes, you are.'

'*You're* stupid.'

'I don't need Mrs Lambert to help me with my reading,' Saoirse says.

A low blow. Róisín has a problem with phonetics. No matter how many hours we spend, flash card after flash card, she struggles. Guesses, which scuppers her comprehension of text. Mrs Lambert assures me she will be fine once she acquires a critical mass of words she recognises by sight. But. The academic doesn't worry me so much as the social. The excuse it gives her sister to claim superiority.

She slips a searching hand into mine, a surreptitious move caught by her sister's magpie eye. Rather than taking the other hand, Saoirse goes for the same one, and it takes much tickling and jiggling and laughter before I have them firmly attached either side.

We arrive thus, a flaxen-topped trio, refugees from early morning sun, into the high grey light of what used be a milking shed, sanitised by whitewash and steel, segregated into pens for ducks, chickens, guinea pigs, rabbits, a couple of random sheep, and Maisie, who is impressively enormous. All competition is forgotten as they stare at her snotty mottled snout chewing hay, two gnarled underfangs making heavy work of it, rhythmically threatening pig cheeks.

'*Wow*,' Róisín says.

'She's huge,' Saoirse says.

'She doesn't look much like a Peppa,' I say. 'I think she's definitely a Maisie.'

'Oh, she's definitely a Maisie,' Michael says.

A rustle of hay on the floor and he is beside us, and I can't figure out if he was there all along or has only walked in now. Usually my radar is set for any sign of him. He stands close. Too close.

Shiver.

'How old is she?' I say.

Because it is all I can think of, and I need to think of something, to deflect his direct look, his amused lips, the light lines framing deep-set blue eyes, set now on my face. A face that may turn traitor.

'She's nearly ten,' he says.

'And is that old or young for a pig?'

Digging deep in my professional small-talk toolbox. A set of skills I'm learning to re-purpose for family gatherings, other awkward situations.

'Kind of middle-aged, I guess. Like us.' He laughs. A laugh that laughs at itself. Invites you along.

'Speak for yourself. I'm only a young thing,'

'What? You mean you're still the right side of forty?'

I whack his check-shirted arm with the back of my fingers.

'Fecking cheek! I have ages to go.'

'Same age as Louisa then?'

'Two years younger.'

'Oh.'

A sudden ripple in the ease. The whirring of calculation. Maybe. Was I even legal? I'm overthinking it.

'You're going great guns with this place.'

'Yep,' he says. 'I've got big plans. The yak arrives next week and we've two alpacas on order.'

'Get you.'

'It's you Dubliners. Coming down here with your notions.'

Our eyes meet in a smile.

'Mochas and lattes and the like, you mean?'

'Exactly. Thinking we're only simple country folk, then giving us all your money for shite.'

I laugh now.

'Aren't you the gombeen man?'

'At least I'm honest about it.'

'Honesty doesn't excuse you. Every criminal I've ever met thinks they're 'honest'. As if owning the fault exonerates them.'

'*Uh* ... exonerate? Schtop there now with them big words, Miss Fancypants Lawyer. Remember, I'm only a simple farm boy.'

Shiver.

Saoirse turns to look at us.

'Mummy, how much does the pig weigh?'

'*Oooh*, she's a big one,' Michael says. 'Well over five hundred pounds. About five times your mammy here.'

Saoirse throws him a sceptical eye, rosehip lips set serious. The stupid part of my brain, the part that is still twelve, sixteen, hopeful, registers the exaggerated maths as a compliment, a flirt, maybe interest. We've danced many versions of this before, over the years, the tentative jokes, the parries, trying to bridge the embarrassment, sweep away what could reasonably be accounted for as an ill-advised drunken fumble between almost children. But. Something today, this morning, in this unlikely space, this domestic tableau, two adults and two children observing a pig, is subtly different. Lighter. New. A shift in him. A shift in me. Maybe the good weather has created an air of hedonism in the universe.

'She smells,' Saoirse says.

'Well, that's morning pig for you. I've just come to muck her out. D'you want to help?'

He waves the bucket in his hand, a carpet of fair hair covering lightly tanned skin, a bald patch near his thumb, a fresh plaster, already stained with blood.

'*Ugh*, no thank you,' Saoirse says.

'Mummy, can we show Maisie to Viva?' Róisín says.

'Viva?'

'Genevieve,' Saoirse says. 'She said to call her Viva. She says everybody does.'

I can feel the lines of me harden, an involuntary reaction. Check myself. I don't know why this girl unsettles me. What visceral sense is alert to her. Whatever it is, I don't like it in me.

'*Viva!*' the children shout.

As if on cue, the girl enters the barn. Viva suits her, an elegant energy that sweeps the space, and my daughters run, jump on her, creating a disturbing effect, like an active art installation of limbs and skin and hair and cotton and denim.

'Well, Viva's a bit of a hit,' Michael says.

The me observing me, observing us, is disgusted at my self-conscious reaction to pull a lock of hair behind my ear, wonder if I still have lipstick on, adjust my stance in my mid-length mammy skirt. The ditsy flower pattern instantly altered. Frowsy.

* * *

The kitchen-slash-living space is abuzz. Folding doors flung open to the garden, granite patio; expensive wooden furniture, colourful cushions and umbrellas to combat the unlikely danger of sunstroke.

Bodies. All shapes and sizes, holding glasses, holding forth, or mooching on the sidelines.

Spinning and whirling newly washed children weaving

through glitz and heels and dye and fake tan and breasts and legs and arms and excess flesh popping from optimistic sizes.

Chinos and Ralph Lauren shirts, sports jackets flung to the side, because the weather is, miraculously, unseasonably warm.

Catering staff, neat in monochrome, wending through the throng with platters of snacks and trays of bubbles.

Helen and Louisa, in clashing florals, coiffed and threaded and hard coloured nails flashing in sunlight like knives.

Sarah, exhausted in an elegant black dress, dark circling her, as if it is all too much effort. Ciarán snotting into her side.

Genevieve – Viva – cool and tanned and blonde-streaked hair, a navy dress with white piping, all young and legs and French.

* * *

Me: Upstairs half an hour earlier, the red Karen Millen, so flattering under shop lights, not quite right. Hitting my hips in the wrong spot.

Gerry, driven demented with questions.

'You look grand,' he'd said. 'They're all grand. Why on earth does it matter anyway? It's a child's Communion.'

But it does. Matter. It shouldn't. Yet it does.

I opt for the back-up option, a demure LK Bennett with what Elena would call darling covered buttons, duck-egg blue. Safe. Pretty. Not sexy.

* * *

Elena fussing, Uncle Brendan in his La-Z-Boy, holding court, a bemused king.

Daniel, all indication of an attempt to sanctify him absent, whining and wheedling, mucky hands hovering at his mother's skirt.

'For ... Daniel, just go out and play with the others!' says Helen. 'Your brothers are in the bouncy castle.'

'But it's my *Communion*, Mammy. Just one more cake, *pleeeease ...*'

A belly already protruding over mini-chinos.

Joe and Ronan and Gerry. Conspiring in a corner with mobile phones. Shades of *The Three Stooges*.

'It's sorted,' Ronan says. 'Brian says the planning will go through this week, my lads say they will be good to go mid-August. Northern fellas. Reliable. You can't get a builder down here for love nor money at the moment.'

Joe and Gerry nodding. Mysterious trips to the bathroom. Lit.

The air heavy and cloying with scents not indigenous to Tullamore.

* * *

Me: hovering on the periphery of a going-nowhere conversation with Helen's family, practising smiley small talk, mining my brain for mutual connection other than the weather. Autopilot. Staged. As if we are all waiting for a director to give instruction for action on a particularly dodgy episode of *Falcon Crest*.

'It's all changed so much,' Sarah says, appearing beside me.

'It has,' I say.

Happy to see her. Concerned at the cut of her. A churn of emotions.

'Granny wouldn't recognise it,' I say.

She's drinking tea, despite the heat. Her soft-lashed eyes pools of sad. I want to hug her. But. Not here. Other barriers.

'Ailish ...'

'Yeah?'

'Just ... I don't ...'

'Is everything okay?'

'I don't know who to ask,'

'You can ask me. Well, if I can be of any help,'

'I'm worried about Ciarán,'

'In what way?'

'He's not reaching his milestones. I'm not being paranoid. Like there's not even one proper word yet. And one of the reasons I keep feeding is because it's the only way to comfort him. He can scream for hours and hours. Lose it so badly he starts banging his head off stuff. It doesn't feel normal. Michael says I'm obsessing, that because he's the only one I'm overprotective, and I am, I know, but I really think there's something wrong. Properly wrong. As a mother you know, don't you?'

I think of little Róisín, sitting on the ground outside, visible in the middle distance, watching all the shenanigans in the bouncy castle. Saoirse in the thick of it.

'Children are like all humans, they come in different shapes and sizes, Sarah,' I say. 'I think they reach so-called milestones in their own time.'

'You think I'm being overprotective?'

'No. I don't. I think you're being a mother. If you're worried, would you not go and get him checked?'

'Michael won't hear of it.'

'Why?'

'I don't know.' She shrugs. Fragility seeping from every pore. 'Fear? We've been through enough. He's been through enough.'

'Well, I reckon it's better to know if there is something, then at least you can get help for the child. They say early intervention is key.'

'Would you talk to him?'

'Who, Michael?'

'Yeah.'

'Me?'

Badum. Badum.

My hand grows slippery on the wine glass.

'Why would Michael talk to me about Ciarán?' I say.

'I don't know. It's just he's always saying what a lovely mother you are with the girls.'

Badum. Badum. Badum, badum, badum.

I laugh.

'But sure he hardly ever sees us.'

'No, but he's right. You are a good mother, so kind and patient. And they're gorgeous little girls. A credit to you.'

Boom.

All the times I've wanted to scream, actually screamed, at my beautiful little girls. The moments when my paper-thin patience wore through. The visceral rawness which, always, hovers beneath.

'You're a great mother, Sarah. You can't doubt or compare yourself to me or anybody else.'

'No, but I'm so worn out, Ailish. I'm not good with words, persuasive with an argument like you are. Would you? Would you have a word with him?'

Briiiing. Briiiing. Briiiiiiiingg.

'I'm not sure it will help?'

'But you'll try? Please. I'm desperate.'

*   *   *

We have cake. A humungous thing, almost as big as the football pitch it represents. Tiny little players, goals, a ball. Offaly jerseys. A source of angst, because Helen insisted on purchasing it from a professional baker, pushing Elena's amateur nose seriously out of joint, producing a politic lack of engagement from those in the know. Which is everybody. Daniel, however, now having devoured everything bar the catering staff, insists on a ceremonial cutting. Helen, Mother of the Communicant, tightly toppling on Jimmy Choos and slurry, calls a messy gathering.

Sacred ritual. Final sacrifice.

Cheering. Whooping.

First blood for Daniel as he plunges a child-unfriendly knife into the pitch with intent, footballer bodies scattered amidst an eruption of chocolate biscuit cake.

Fizz, buzz, more champagne for the adults.

'Where's Ciarán?' Michael says.

Sarah, still beside me, jumps. Lightning panic.

'I thought he was with you?'

A ripple. Confusion. A whisper, slow at first, gathering pace. Energy. Volume.

'*Ciarán? Ciarán? CIARÁN!*'

Seconds morph into minutes. Adults shout. Children shout. Scatter. A haphazard army.

'How far can a two-year-old go?'

Elena takes charge, crisis management.

'He can't be far, check the garden, towards the gate first. Somebody check upstairs. He likes small spaces.'

I head towards the old part of the house, carpeted stairs, reimagined original features.

'*Ciarán? CIARÁN!*'

Michael coming up the stairs behind me. Me, conscious of my gait. The smooth rippling lines of this dress. Manolo Blahniks making tidy impressions on deep pile wool carpet. All these rooms of my childhood. All the doors. Sliding doors.

'She should have been keeping an eye on him,' Michael says.

'He's your child too.'

'No, I know ... I just ... oh for fuck's sake – *CIARÁN!*'

A shout from downstairs.

'We have him!'

Michael's face, crumbling.

'Oh, thank God.'

My hand already on the handle of the door to the room which used to be 'my room'. Already pushing it open.

Genevieve.

Viva.

Joe.

Jesus!

I slam the door.

* * *

I slam the boot of the Volvo down hard, wrestle with the bags.

'Genevieve, will you get the girls inside?'

Less life in her now. More sullen strop.

* * *

The girls absorb the atmosphere, whine all the way home. Gerry and I tight-lipped, avoiding each other's glances.

'Maisie was the best bit,' Róisín says.

'The yak will be better,' Saoirse says.

'I will still like Maisie the best.'

'A yak will be cool. Maisie is just a smelly old pig.'

'Well, I don't care. She's my friend.'

'She's a *pig*. You're so stupid sometimes, Róisín.'

'Not stupid. You're stupid.'

'Stupid, stupid, stupid …'

'*Stop it.* That word is banned. If I hear either of you use it again you're grounded for a week.' Like this is a dire consequence for seven-year-olds.

Genevieve is quiet.

Saoirse makes a damp attempt to sing '*Allouette*'. Stops.

* * *

Getting undressed for bed the previous night.

'Maybe you didn't see what you thought you saw?' Gerry says.

A hushed conversation as he helps me undo those damn buttons on my dress.

'Maybe they were looking for Ciarán too?'

'Are you sticking up for Joe? I can't believe you'd stick up for that *prick*. He was always a fucking sleeveen. He had his hand up her skirt, Gerry. They were kissing. Up against the wall. Lord knows what else.'

'Well, it takes two to tango …'

'For fuck's sake, you *are* taking his side.'

'There are no sides, Ailish,'

'Tell that to Helen.'

'Ah, here now, you can't go interfering in his marriage …'

'I should have known – your cosy little cartel – all the big men, you and him and *Ronan*. Thinking you're all property magnates, living the fucking Hollywood dream. Was he next? Were you? Is that place even an au pair agency? Are we all hiring prostitutes into our houses?'

'*Shush*, you're hysterical, people will hear.'

* * *

He won't sleep on the floor so I sleep on the seam of the mattress. I don't sleep. I seethe. He sleeps.

Joe. Always a nasty little fucker.

Genevieve. *Viva.* Whore.

* * *

After slamming the door:

Michael. At the other end of the house, Brendan and Elena's room.

'Say nothing,' he'd said.

Like I would go down and denounce them amidst the rubble of cake and cards and fifty-euro notes sticking out from Daniel's back pocket.

'We can't just ignore it,' I say. 'Helen needs to know.'

'Why?'

'What?'

'Why does she need to know?'

'Her husband's a cheating bastard.'

'Do you think she doesn't know this already?'

'What?'

'Look, Joe has been my friend for more years than I can remember, and he has many admirable qualities, but fidelity isn't one of them.'

He reaches for my hand. I pull it away. Sharply. Nauseous now.

'Ailish, I'm not condoning it, I'm just saying that's the way it is ...'

'Why does she stay with him?'

'She has five sons. Their lives are tied up in the farm. There would be a custody battle, it would be messy.'

'But he's a cheating bastard.'

'She likes the trappings. The car, the golf club membership, the holidays. Hard to give all that up.'

'Those things don't make you happy. They just paper over cracks.'

I think of Helen, mascara globbing round tired, yellowed eyes, the wine glass that grows from her fingers.

'Look, we'll talk about it. Not now, let's just get today out of the way. Really, it's none of our business.'

'She's my au pair – that kind of makes it my business, don't you think?'

'No. I don't. But we'll talk.'

* * *

'It's not working out.' I say.

We stand in the spare room, her meagre clothing in neat piles on the bed, cheap make-up on the desk. Only a fledgling woman.

'Mrs Kennedy, I ... what you saw ...' Her eyes are tear-tired.

I am unmoved.

'Pack your bags, Genevieve.'

* * *

My phone pings.

You okay?

Define okay.

Did you say anything to Gerry?

Of course I did.

What did he say?

I told Genevieve to leave.

She's gone back to France?

I don't care where she's gone. She's not here anymore.

Are you okay?

I don't know what that means. 'Okay'.

Do you want to chat?

About Joe and his infidelities? I think I know all I need to, thanks.

I'm not going to make excuses for him.

Then why do we need to chat?

I'd like to.

21

The sun beats hot on my traitorous head as I walk up Nassau Street. Pass tourists with maps and backpacks, pouring into and out of Trinity College. Turn the corner onto Grafton Street, Molly Malone and her wheelbarrow, a sea of skin in various stages of raddle, the smell of suncream and greasy McDonald's styrofoam, which permeates. A hazy film hanging on vaporous heat. Hedonistic heels sailing past collection hats praying for a couple of euros. Flower-sellers optimistically shouting their wares, keen to make bank before their product withers. Brown Thomas and Marks and Spencer sparkling promise, renewal, magic to those in the know. In the money. Humanity in every hue, striving against concrete and glass and gold-stencilled lettering.

Everything: fizzing.

* * *

Me: heavy and light in navy and white, a new patterned dress from Tommy Hilfiger, belted at the waist, pretty-chic but maybe casual, strappy wedge sandals, a straw bag I acquired years ago. In Paris, I think. Hair loose, make-up natural. Trying to belie the churn in my stomach. My conniving head.

* * *

Lunch: Bewley's. In plain sight. A legitimate and verified excuse. A family member, helping another family member.

Into the yawn of the high ceilings, the certainty of mahogany and brass, Harry Clarke's stained glass creations casting dust motes of colour and shadow.

Michael is sitting at a table for two. Stands. Half stands. Smiles. Waves a hand for me to sit.

I do. I smile. A tentative thing.

What the fuck am I doing?

'You look beautiful,' he says.

The wrong word. It shocks. It jars. I know immediately it is wrong, but it is only later I will realise why. All these years in my head I've imagined this moment, him saying, again:

'*You're lovely.*'

Because somehow in my head *lovely* is what?

Wholesome?

Not *perverse*.

Beautiful is too much, too far, too generic. A word every woman wants to hear, a word a man will use to tell her she has been seen, often before he lures her to bed.

Is that why I'm here? Is that not why I'm here? That is why I am here.

I struggle not to shake. Fight to control my hands.

'Get you,' I say. 'Acting all sophisticated just 'cos you're up in the Big Schmoke now.'

He laughs.

Doesn't blink.

'You do,' he says. 'Look beautiful.'

Smiles again.

* * *

We've been texting for weeks. My discreet little work Nokia, tiny gold bar of deceit. Beestings of data exchange, electronic packets of treachery, tickling the edges of plausible deniability. Friend or flirt? A good barrister could argue either. Every ping a dopamine hit. Sitting in work, an uncontrollable smile. Waiting for a response, a barely contained sweat. Steve, across the partition, sipping coffee, looking suspicious. On the DART, emoting at my phone, quick-fire responses. Minding my phone, leaving it in my bag, lest Gerry notice a stray message that begs a question. The sharp and bitter justifying taste of would-he-care-anyway thoughts. So caught up is he in his clients, Lakeview conundrums, dodgy dealings with dodgy men. Other reasons. Undercurrents I'm too tired to explore.

Lulls in the exchange send me wild. What is he doing? In the shop? Mucking out Maisie? Playing with Ciarán, putting him to bed? Making love to Sarah? The world only bearable again because there's a ping:

Hey, CityChick.
Hey, FarmBoy.
What you doin'?
Playing taxidriver. Piano with Róisín. Saoirse at GAA. Usual
Thursday madness. You?
Babysitting Ciarán.

I restrain myself from correcting the common male tendency
to compare minding one's own child to the equivalent of an
adolescent chore which could, should, be something undertaken
for pocket money. I might correct it in another. But. Amn't I
guilty too, *taxi driver*? As if we were, are, intended for better.
Two of us in it. Instead, my thumb taps:

Where's Sarah?
In bed.
Is she okay?
I don't know what that means. Okay.

We have playnames and tics and in-jokes, a language of our
own, a blanket we've been pretending is organic, been weaving
with purpose.

Touché. But why is she in bed in the middle of the day?
She says she's tired. Has had enough.
Of?
Everything.
Specifically?

Ciarán. She says she can't handle him. She's exhausted.

Is he okay?

Asleep. Now.

You need to talk to her about Ciarán. You need to talk to somebody about him.

She won't talk to me.

She wants to, she told me at the Communion, she's worried about him.

It just ends up in a row. The child is fine. She's a mess.

She asked me to talk to you.

So. Let's talk, CityChick.

Isn't that what we're doing? Talking?

* * *

Scurried phone calls. Three, arranged in advance. Stolen evenings when I tell Gerry I can't stand it anymore, need to get out for a walk. For air. Leave him to *babysit* his children. How easily I lie. Me, who has committed the exterior, at least, of my life to the upholding of truth. I shroud it now in complicated folds and layers, barking at my girls:

'For God's sake, can I not have a little privacy?'

My head full of this FarmBoy. Dreams which spill from restless nights while Gerry soft-snores into daytime, snatched or engineered idle moments when I imagine conversations, weave threads of connection into story, fantasise about his farm-hardened body, then and now, all the ways we might give to and receive from each other pleasure. Mental. Physical. Sweet release. A moment, moments, to render all the other not so pleasurable moments, insignificant.

> Let's meet. Talk properly.
> About Ciarán?
> What else?
> I'm serious.
> So am I.
> You're lovely.
> Stop that.
> Only if you stop being lovely.

* * *

The swimming run, chlorine soaked by the pool, watching the girls gently, chiding them into showers and clothes and drying hair all manageable, joyful, fun now. Me, a better mother, a better human, because somebody – no, not *somebody* – Michael – thinks I am lovely.

Lovely. Such a non-specific word.

It can be interpreted so many ways.

It could be: seen, liked.

Or: Appreciated.

Maybe: Loved?

This is not, cannot be, what he means. It's too soon, too sudden. After twenty-odd years.

Lovely.

Maybe not so wholesome.

* * *

I'm in Dublin on Tuesday. Can we meet?
Next Tuesday?
The very one.
I'm working.
We could go for dinner?

Dinner. Babysitters, blow-dry, heels. A glass or two of wine.
The potential for abandon.

I could meet you for lunch?
Okay. Lunch so.

* * *

Beautiful.

We sit, stand, on this line. Wobbling. Unsure of its nature
and whether we can, could, will, cross it. Knowing, absolutely,
we shouldn't. One toe in the wrong direction, we detonate.
Blow up all the lives. But the look he gives me is hungry.

'So,' he says.

'So.'

'Here we are.'

'Here we are indeed.'

'You look ...'

'Yeah, you said.'

Smiles. Thin. Ironic. A meeting at the eyes.

'We should get food,' he says.

We take turns to go up to the counter, me first, a salad, a yoghurt. Him, sausages and chips, beans. Sparkling water, a Coke.

Me, conscious of the eyes, the other customers. Dublin is, at its core, a village.

'So,' I say.

Smiles.

'Did you tell Sarah we were meeting?'

'Sarah and I aren't talking much at the moment.'

I fiddle with a napkin. The weight of Sarah on me. Her happiness in my hands.

Brrrinnggg.

Shush.

'Did you tell Gerry?' he says.

I didn't. Gerry and I aren't talking much either at the moment, but I don't say this. How I tell my husband I'm lonely, how he hears this as a whinge, an extra pull on his already exhausted resources. Another chore. A void he may be incapable of filling anyway.

Lonely.

Lovely.

'I told my mother,' I say.

'Established an alibi?'

'Something like that.'

'You CityChick lawyers sure are devious.'

'It's just ...'

'What?'

'This is Dublin. There are eyes everywhere ...'

He side-eye sweeps the room, melodramatically. I laugh.

'There are *eyes everywhere*?' he says.

'Oh, you know what I mean.'

'I do?'

'I'm not sure what we're up to here.'

'We're having lunch.'

I swat him with the napkin.

'We're family, having lunch, chatting about family things,' he says. 'There doesn't have to be anything more. We're friends.'

I digest the shape and form of this: friends. What this 'friendship' might look like. He stares at me.

'Anyway,' I say. 'About Ciarán.'

'What about Ciarán?'

'How's he doing?'

His face sets serious. A shadow pause.

'I think you might be right.' he says,

Slow, hard syllables.

'In what way?'

'Since Sarah ... since the Communion, I've had him with me a lot more. I've ... there's stuff ...'

'What sort of stuff?'

'He has no words yet.'

'None?'

'No. It's like he's not even trying or ... interested? And he bangs his head. Off the floor, off the wall. Like you think everything is fine and then he loses it, zero to ninety in a split second.'

'So, Sarah's not wrong?'

A different shadow. A twitch.

'She said you had some problems with Róisín?'

'Have. Not had. Not problems. Some challenges. She just needs a little extra help. It's child-specific, though. I can give you the number of somebody who might be able to point you in the right direction.'

'Thanks. I'd appreciate that.'

'Well, I'd like to help. If I can. You guys have been through so much.'

'You really are lovely, you know?'

Some feral alert: What happened to beautiful? I'm lovely now – as in, good mother? What happened to girl I've been fantasising about for years and would still like to fuck? Is that fantasy only mine? Am I merely another random woman, maybe one of a string of random women – beautiful – *lovely* – whom he goes to when perfect Sarah starts to fray?

Brrriinnnngggg ...

I don't know this man before me at all. His history, his morals, his immorals. The inner self he clearly keeps hidden from the outer world.

I don't know me at all either.

Brrrrringgggg ...

'How's *Joe?*' I say.

The irony not lost on me that, sitting here, a married woman, with my cousin's husband, sitting here *flirting* with – *seducing?* – my cousin's husband, I am in no position to judge Joe.

'You heard?' he says.

'Heard what?'

'About Genevieve?'

'What about Genevieve?'

'Sorry, I shouldn't ...'

All awkward now.

'What about Genevieve?' I say.

'No, really, not my business. I just thought Gerry would have told you.'

'Told me what? Michael, you have to tell me now.'

He shifts, the flirtspace altered now. Invaded by an invisible gas.

'She was pregnant,' he says.

'Pregnant?'

'She said it was Joe's.'

Smack. Panic. Smack.

Briiiiiiiiinnnnnnngggg ...

'She contacted him looking for money.'

Boom.

'What?'

'Look, sorry, I shouldn't have said anything. I thought Gerry would have ... he was like a sort of liaison between them.'

'*What the fuck?*'

'I know.'

'Why didn't he say anything to me?'

Breathe.

'I don't know. Look, it's sorted.'

'Sorted?'

'Well ...'

He hesitates. Looks embarrassed. Plays with his knife.

'I think she's had an abortion.'

I think of the frail frame of the girl I ran from my house. Standing over her in judgement.

Me.

'Is she okay?'

'I don't know, I think so. Look, it got a bit messy – maybe she wasn't pregnant, maybe she was just looking for money. Gerry and Joe sorted it. You know what girls like that are like.'

Boom.

'Girls like what?'

'*Uh*, Ailish, leave it?'

Breathe.

'No. I won't leave it. Girls like *what?*'

'Look, she's probably done this before. Thinks nothing of it.'

Breathe.

'Girls don't have abortions and think nothing of it.'

I realise I'm raising my voice incrementally.

All flirting finished.

'No, look, I know,' he says. 'And I realise it's upsetting. When I think of all Sarah and I have been through trying to have a child, and you're such a good mother with your girls. Look it's just one of those things. Maybe she wasn't even pregnant at all. I'm sorry I said anything.'

* * *

I stand at the school gates, waiting for a bus to drop my girls back from summer camp. Watch them spill down the steps, thrilled to see me, the other mothers trying not to stare at them.

Infinitely watchable, my mirror-image children. And yet, me, I always have half an eye on the ghost sibling who trails them. Sometimes a boy, sometimes a girl, grown now, twenty-two, sometimes resembling me, the girls, sometimes Michael, sometimes Ciarán.

Ethereal, structureless, but always there.

'What's your relationship with Michael like now?' the woman says.

'He's my cousin's husband.'

'He never found out? Never suspected?'

'I'm not sure what he knows. If he knows anything, he never seemed to make the connection. He appears to be one of those men who can walk away without consequences. As if the rules don't apply to them.'

'You sound bitter.'

'Only with myself. For not recognising it. For seeing who I wanted to see in front of me, not who was actually there.'

'And if you'd got together with him …?'

'Later? Ever? It would have been a disaster. He just became fixed in my head, you know, as The Fix. To the greater problem.'

'You've resolved that now?'

'Resolved? No. I don't think I'll ever pull all those strands together, make sense of it. I'm resigned to it, maybe.'

Breathe.

'It's such a loss, isn't it?'

'What is?'

'The longing.'

22

December 2016

'They want to replace it,' Barbara says.

Her leg is raised on a pouffe. I'm unwinding Frank's loose bandage-work, tentatively uncovering the offending knee, which reeks of Deep Heat, armed with a support sock the chemist dolefully suggested *might* help.

'You never said,' I say.

'I'm saying now.'

'When did they say this to you?'

'The last time your daddy and I were in with them.'

Which I think is about a week ago. Feel guilty for not knowing exactly. For assuming Frank could handle the detail of it.

'Have they said when?'

The pain is constant now, her mobility severely limited. It's showing in the house. Thick black scars of built-up food remnants on the hob, the high waft of two-week out-of-date ham I remove from the fridge, which I guiltily suspect Frank has still been feeding them. The air of dust and dusk that sweeps the cold brown and beige edges on a sunny December day.

'No, I suppose I'm on a waiting list, like everybody else. I expect it could be years. *Ooh*, careful. *Oooh, ooh, ooh …*'

The skin on her legs is crackle-dry and gossamer-thin. I move a nail awkwardly close to a might-be-ulcer and the tissue splits easily, spills a thin line of blood.

'*Aaah,* Ailish …'

'Sorry, sorry, sorry.'

I reach into my pocket for a tissue but there is none, go to the downstairs bathroom for toilet roll. The bowl is stained and reeks of dried piss, an ancient bar of Imperial Leather, cracked and shot through with dirt, the sink caked in its powdery residue.

'Mum …' I say.

She holds her Brendella skirt, as old as I am, nervous as a virgin above the soft grey-white flesh of her thigh, the ridges and warp of her hands – which are my hands, older and arthritic – braced for anticipated pain. Miss Havisham on her wedding night. I pull the sock on over yellowed toenails, a misshapen foot, up the pop-veined leg, as gently as I can, which is not all that gently.

'Have you considered,' I say, 'getting a cleaning lady? Just for the minute, while you're out of action with the knee?'

'Frank wouldn't hear of it – *oooh*, Ailish, careful, careful …'

'Did he say that?'

'Say what?'

'Say that he doesn't want a cleaning lady?'

'Oh, Ailish, don't be silly. Cleaning lady? How much would

that cost? On a pension? We're doing fine. I can still do a bit, on my good days. I'll be flying once this thing is sorted. Cleaning ladies aren't for the likes of us. Sure they'd have nothing to do. Frank wouldn't hear of it.'

Frank's hearing is increasingly part of the problem. I catch him often now, mid-stare, a nonsensical answer to a straightforward question. He'll shake his grey hair, throw a hopeful filmy eye at me and turn up a hearing aid so discreet he keeps losing it, join the conversation almost normally. Almost. And I know this is how it happens. I've watched it with friends and their parents, the slow demise of one partner, the despair of the other. Ever-decreasing circles. The aren't-we-lucky-to-have-our-parents-still of women who look ten years older than they should. Lives reduced to soundbites and prayers, cleaning piss and shit-stained folds of skin and endless rounds of hospital visits. The constant expectation the phone might ring, all plans tentative.

I know there is no point in arguing. My mother will agree to paid help if and when and in her own time. But. I spent the first two hours here cleaning out the fridge, running a cloth around the kitchen, sweeping and mopping floors and now I need to add bathrooms to my list.

'That's too tight,' she says.

'It's supposed to be tight. To give you support.'

She squirms stiffly in the chair, as if to underscore the great weight of her suffering.

'I suppose I'll give it a try.'

I call by at least once a week, usually while I'm en route somewhere for work or off to something related to the girls. I'm calculating now my capacity for a second or third – longer – visit. Reflect with no small degree of selfishness that their demise is coinciding nicely with the girls learning to drive, going to college. Just when I thought I was coming near the end of The Game of Dependents, there is another, more advanced level. One that requires the same weary skillset: driver, nurse, skivvy. Extra firepower.

Inevitability seeps like the fractured, dissipating light refracting through the windows, which need a good wash. A slow, inescapable, torturous suffocation, especially when, in my other portfolio, I have the Leaving Cert this year. By two.

We talk like this. The Mammies.

'*Can't* at the moment,' we say. '*We* have the *Leaving Cert.*'

And we close our doors and fuster around our befuddled children, as if we can control and fix this for them too.

My children, technically adults now, are divine but tetchy creatures who get on each other's nerves, steal clothes, confuse boyfriends, compete for friend groups. Chicks desperate to fly, who will hatch fully when in possession of a driving license, a race that is fierce and bitter, and will only intensify when they have to share the shiny red Mini Cooper their father presented them with for their eighteenth birthday. Without consulting me. An assumption of stupendous proportion, which says much about The State of Our Marriage.

Gerry, colour-drained and himself, shiny pate and enlarged pores, careering manfully towards his half-century, doesn't get it. Or maybe he does, considers the adulation of his daughters worth the price.

'I thought you'd be delighted, a nice surprise for you too. Now they won't be looking for your car all the time,' he says.

'We could have discussed it? You know what they're like – they can't share breakfast never mind their keys to freedom.'

Of course, I will be the one called upon to mediate, because my husband, after so many years of marriage, is still hardly ever here.

And here is not where it used to be.

Here is wall-to-wall chrome and glass, halfway up Killiney Hill, overlooking Dalkey. A vista of navigable sea, ferries and sailboats, a neighbour who paddleboards on smooth surface days. A standalone bargain in 2011, when prices plummeted, the market was flooded with abandoned dreams and few battle-brave buyers.

Here is wide and air-filled, perpetual clean lines, ideal for entertaining Gerry's clients and cronies, ritual gatherings with his wider family, and the ubiquitous Moira, widowed six years, dining out on her son's reputation now.

Here is a vision of success, which maybe once belonged to some version of me.

This me feels slight as air, walking through rooms that are too big to be cosy, with furniture and art that doesn't feel of my choosing, though of course I had a hand in it, a nose wrinkled when a designer put swatches of curtain material in front of me, threw colour options on a wall, gave advice on where to hang paintings. And maybe I justified it for the sake of the girls. After all, this parenting lark is one of continuous improvement. Or is it one-upmanship? I don't know anymore. My girls feel inferior to nobody. This was the goal. Stated, unstated. And maybe all the *stuff* stuff used to sit well with me. Some days I am so embroiled in the South County Dublin dream, a constant reaching for some bar of respectability, acceptability, I struggle to find any version of me I want to own.

* * *

My workdays are consumed now with immigration work, an impossible soup of paperwork, endless bureaucracy and authority stonewalling. If you have money, resource to produce documents that look authentic, then it is time and frustration. If you are a human caught in Direct Provision, with no support from your nation state, you're pretty much fucked. And it's here I'm finding purpose. One day a week when I do pro bono work with unfortunates caught in Clondalkin Towers or Mosney. Mothers and children and men who've lost hope, looking at the world through cynical eyes. A slalom of compounding cultural issues. An endurance test of small wins and large setbacks.

I come home to my mausoleum of granite and marble and light and drink wine with stones in my stomach.

'I'd like to set up my own practice,' I say.

'What do you want to do that for?' Gerry says.

'I don't know. Redress the balance? Give something back? Mostly pro bono work, only take enough paying clients to pay for it. I know the system now, I'm steeped in it. I'm good at it.'

'But you wouldn't earn anything?'

'Just a basic salary. How much do we need? Is all this not enough?'

Gerry is his father's son: public paragon, presentable husband, a politic intelligence honed in the style of a rodent barrister, forever on the lookout for the next buck. Where others see a straight path, Gerry sees sliding doors, backdoors, escape hatches and opportunities. It took me time to realise this about my husband. These qualities obscured behind his affable front. Perhaps I wanted to believe the self he portrayed as much he wanted to believe the one I did – good girl, competent woman, devoted mother. Facades which have worn over time like our faces, truer selves emerging as experience erodes and etches its lines. We are survivors, Gerry and I. When Lakeview turned Shitshow at the height of the recession, he'd had the foresight to channel our borrowings through a limited company. Joe, Ronan and even Michael shouldered enormous personal debt, while we came through relatively unscathed. Gerry got tribunal work through a contact of his father, and where others sweated and scrimped to pay utility bills and mortgages, lost property and possessions and face, our bank account never flatlined. Did remarkably well, considering.

But still. He's like a squirrel saving nuts for an apocalypse. He won't give up my salary – our baseline income – easily. So he hums and haws and pretends to give my proposal due deliberation. He's not against it, in principle, he says. He will get back to me. He needs to consider how it might play in the 'larger narrative'.

'Of course, you know Ailish wants to be a *human rights lawyer*,' Moira says.

At a drinks reception before a memorial dinner for his father in the Shelbourne. News of our chat on the wind now, because, well, they're like that, Gerry and his mummy.

'Just like Amal Clooney,' she says.

Wrinkles and suspect age spots and long dried-out hair, jostling with satin and sequins, a dress that cost the price of feeding a family in Zimbabwe for a year. Teeth rotting benignly under a startling red lipstick, itself mid-migration into crevices and clefts. The face of a successful life. The face of my future, a version of my face that proactively haunts me, prompts the purchase of expensive remedies in airports, hours spent in front of the bathroom mirror, poking and plucking and massaging, as if I can buy kindness from time.

Conscious it is running out.

An image of my neighbour on his paddleboard, skimming the depths of the middle distance, comfortable with risk, the uncertainty of his voyage acceptable. Maybe exciting.

But. I'm not that paddleboarder.

The tracks of my life feel rigid and set, unspecified weeks, months, years left to serve in purgatory before I can contemplate a horizon.

23

We do Christmas in our house, this house, now. Four Christmas trees, a million fripperies and pointless presents. Moira and the girls organise most of the fuss. Gerry is on turkey duty, I take veg and starters. Frank and Barbara come and go by taxi. Moira and Gerry sometimes invite randomers, the odd widowed judge or well-connected visitor from abroad. This year, it's an old friend of Gerry's father, a man formerly of some influence in legal spheres, Brian, and his wife Jean. People of enough import to excite Moira to purchase new table linen for us. An early 'gift'.

Since the Christmas exams, Saoirse has been partying, Róisín is still at the books. Both are interested in law, and probably both will get it in some form. It would be easier if they wanted to do different things, but I suspect they think it will please us, and, well, it's in them. There's a points gap in their academic performance, narrowing now that it's down to graft. I'm hoping Róisín's hard work will pay off for her. She's still the softer twin, the one who will pick up a low mood in me and try to soothe it with a cuddle.

The low moods come and go. They irritate Gerry, who doesn't understand them, thinks I'm happy if we're having sex, talks therapists and antidepressants when we're not. Doesn't get the complexity of it, realise that sometimes more sex is a bad sign. Sometimes it is merely a bid to feel *something*, and sometimes what I feel is only sadness. That I've tried this and everything and anything I can think might help, and my greatest fear is that maybe the emptiness at the core of me doesn't want to be filled. Resists all notion of it, as if to own some sort of comfort would be too good for me. Beneath the glossy exterior, the pictures of us in *VIP Magazine* at some worthy event, the tended hair and tailored clothes and expensive smiles, the heart of me is still leaden. In a quiet head moment the slightest prompt can send me spiralling, back to thoughts of Barbara, as though we are inextricably tied in some pact of grief, of penance. The Trip to England. A tumour in the story of us, malignant and festering, an ever-present potential to erupt, spill its poison. Only tentatively contained.

* * *

My mother sits awkwardly amidst the fairy-lit Christmas Day twilight of our living space, champagne eschewed, a Harvey's Bristol Cream in her hand. Her hair is yesterday-set and she's wearing a best dress, a burgundy affair of delicately appliquéd top and pleated skirt, falling below the mangled knee when standing, exposing pink-bandaged fallibility under wrinkle-skin tights when she sits. Her long-suffering feet are sorely encased in black patent leather courts, their wide-fit not wide enough to contain an accumulation of fluid, a barometer I monitor constantly, a visible indication of invisible threats, a puzzle to be overthought in slow moments. Despite age and experience, she is still out of her depth with people she considers 'quality', such as Moira and her mates today, unsure of her footing, watchful of some idiom that might mark her as not belonging. I recognise this, I think, because it's in me too. This feeling that the spaces of your life are an ill fit. But her front never slips. Some days I wonder if she remembers at all. If 1985 is my fanciful figment alone, a story I tell myself to atone for the fortune in my life. Or explain it. Balances and checks. A cold clutch of menopause-addled breath at the thought of my devil-dealing, what pacts might I have made when out of my mind?

But no. My daughters could never have been born of any kind of badness. They shine with truth – a hopeful new generation, minds opening like flowers, only expecting sun. Our love for them so fierce it could – has – created a world where everything is fair and right. They are the fix.

We gather round my mother. Saoirse and I assist her to navigate crutch and knee, limp-shuffle soft across slippery oak from sofa to dining area.

'Good woman,' I say. 'You're doing great.'

Róisín brings up the rear with Frank, a happy bemused head on him, but still recognisably himself, and I wonder in a heartsore moment if this is because he was always somewhat absent. If this is a pattern in my life. Amorphous men. Creatures I can't quite gain purchase on.

* * *

We make everybody comfortable, fill the Waterford Crystal with wine and water. Moira, useless to me in terms of practical help now her friends are here, is in full flight of reminiscence. Who knew who and where they are now, what they are doing, if they are anywhere at all. A large amount of them are it seems, like Gerry's father, deceased. The trio present tales of colourful characters and hijinks from days when social limits were looser and tighter in different ways. I catch the girls' eyes in wry amusement when Moira calls one of Gerry's father's ex-colleagues a 'raving homosexual' in a derogatory way, shake my head smally. We've had this conversation and, though the girls don't get it, they do.

We wait table, the four of us, expert quick-fire rounds of plates and bowls and bottles back and forth to the kitchen. My parents quiet, stiff smiles, amidst all the chatter. It turns out that Jean is active in the Citizen's Assembly, a subject which fascinates and dominates the media at the moment because of the upcoming Repeal the Eight referendum. A favourite topic of argument amongst my girls and their friends. A subject that invariably sends me mute to dark recesses of the past, humming in my head, jaw clenched. An autonomic response I'm aware of, my curious eye covertly riveting on my mother. Blank as a wall.

The debate gains traction alongside the sprouts. Is fuelled through the trifle with liberal glasses of Sauvignon Blanc.

'It's obviously a very emotive topic,' Jean says.

'We shouldn't even be debating it,' Saoirse says. 'It's our right to choose, to have access to proper healthcare.'

'Well, in cases like Savita Halappanavar, it's very clear-cut,' Gerry says.

'It's never clear cut,' Moira says. 'It's a baby, a life.'

'I think in case of rape or cases like Savita's, where there's urgent medical need, then there should be no question,' Róisín says.

'You'll end up with abortion on demand,' says Moira. 'Nobody will take responsibility.'

'It *is* taking responsibility,' Saoirse says. 'Having a child you can't look after is irresponsible.'

'There should be better access to all forms of contraception,' Gerry says.

'The morning after pill should be given without prescription,' Róisín says.

'We should have the right to choose,' Saoirse says. 'It's about autonomy over our bodies. Nobody should be forced to have a child they don't want.'

'Nobody should have to travel for healthcare,' Róisín says.

'Like in our Ailish's day when they had to take her to Manchester,' Frank says.

'Don't mind him,' my mother says. 'He's getting all confused.'

'We've always insisted with the girls there should be no secrets,' you say. 'There is nothing so bad it would ever need to be hidden. It's what you say to children, isn't it? In case of kiddie-fiddlers, or something. You want them to be able to come to you and tell you anything. So you can protect them.'

'Secrets aren't always bad,' the woman says.

'How do you mean?'

'Sometimes they are protection.'

24

We wave the guests and my parents off in taxis. Gerry, his mother, the girls and I. Stand, motionless, in the double-height space. Poul Henningsen artichoke chandeliers throwing orange light and shade on soft brown suede Denelli sofas. More Halloween than Christmas. Spooky silhouettes against the sparkly view, invisible from the outside. Still a stage.

I think of our neighbour and his paddleboard. Imagine him industriously making his way over grey-glass sea towards a cold moon.

'Can I have a word, Ailish?' Gerry says.

A trace of barrister tone, prompting me to defence. Defiance. Wine-brave.

'About what?' I say.

'You know what.'

'How can I know if you don't tell me?'

'Not here.'

'Why not here?'

A swift movement of his eyes, a tug-frown, as if he is

remonstrating with one of the children in front of other parents. Doesn't want to yell, cause a scene.

'Maybe we should leave it until tomorrow. You've had a skinful,' he says.

'I've had no more than you, no more than them.'

I wave towards the girls, who have been drinking all day too, on the sly. His mother.

'Exactly, we're not in the right space for this. Let's leave it,' he says.

'No. Let's not. What is your problem, Gerry? Something wrong with the soup?'

'You know what the fucking problem is.'

'I don't. Know. What. The. Fucking. Problem. Is. Tell me.'

'Leave it.'

'No.'

'Not in front of the children. Girls go to bed. Mum, you too.'

'I'm not going to bed,' Moira says. 'You can't tell me to go to bed, Gerry. What is wrong with you?'

'See, even your mother doesn't know.'

'My mother has selective hearing.'

'I do not have selective hearing,' Moira says.

'Stop it, guys,' Róisín says.

'Why are you being like this?' Saoirse says. 'Stop it. You're ruining Christmas.'

The paddleboarder in my head enters a liquid moon-shadow, dips his oar in the water once, twice, changing sides, forcibly pushing at the ripples, the navy line of horizon nigh.

'You're making a big deal out of nothing,' I say.

'It's not nothing,' Gerry says.

He sounds unsure now.

The paddleboarder U-turns, lines himself up to head back to the shore.

'I don't know what's eating you, Gerry, but I agree we're all a bit drunk, and the girls are getting upset – let's go to bed, start again tomorrow,' I say.

'We're all very tired,' Moira says. 'It's been such a lovely day, let's not spoil it. If you're getting all worked up about that stupid remark Frank made, Gerry, then relax – the man is clearly demented. Ailish never had an abortion.'

'You didn't, Mum, did you?' Róisín says.

Her face, her sweet face, puzzled.

I pause a second too long.

And we're too long a couple not to read invisible signs, the sublanguage we sometimes mistake for complacency. My face, frozen.

A tiny twitch.

Gerry.

His face twisted.

'Did you? Did you abort my child? Ailish?'

'Stop it, Gerry, you're making this all about you. As fucking usual. I did not abort your child.'

Everybody sober now.

25

Day 1

Me: small in the kitchen, high stool, silk dressing gown adrift, back of thigh exposed, tacky to cream Italian leather. Coffee. My third.

Sea: a struggling early sun, dripping diamonds on blue-grey sea-ice, tickling the underside of a ferry.

Sky: smudgy. Undecided.

'You okay?' Saoirse says.
A hug.

Day 3

Eyes: leaky with grief.
    All of it.

'It's a lot to process, Ailish,' Gerry says, 'I need a few days just to straighten my head.'

A suitcase: larger than it needs to be.

Day 4

'Your dad is getting very confused, Ailish,' Barbara says.

Sink: dirty strainer, green and mouldy with the odour of damp teabags.

'I think we need to talk to Dr O'Brien,' Barbara says.

Day 7

'Fiona?'

'Ailish?'

'Hey. How are you?'

'God, it's been ages. Yeah, we're all good. Is everything okay?'

'No.'

No. It is not.

Day 10

'Ailish?' Moira says. 'How are you doing? Listen, I've been speaking to Jean – you remember her from Christmas? – about all the upset. She's quite progressive on these things. She'd like to talk to you.'

Day 12

'Is Dad coming back?' Róisín says.

To the high ceiling, the room, the view.

Day 15

Me: lamplit, cross-legged and crinkled, on the rug.

Sea: rhythmic ripples of light.

Paddleboarder: absent.

Wine bottle: empty.

Glass:
>   slow motion shadows,
>>   flying across the room …

Day 16

Front door: *click, clunk.* Wheels on wood.

Day 22

Me: making omelettes.

'There's a fee for the mocks, we need to pay it today,' Róisín says.

'I thought we'd paid it already?' Gerry says.

'No, we paid the fee for the actual exams already,' Saoirse says. 'This is different.

'Always another way to get money out of us,' Gerry says.

Table: porridge, berries, toast – wholegrain, avocado, coffee.

'You're meeting Jean today?' Gerry says.

'Who's Jean?' Saoirse says.

'You know. The woman from Christmas, Granny's friend, the Citizen's Assembly lady,' Róisín says.

'I am,' I say.

26

Jean and I meet in Avoca off the N7, a modern airy space filled with spindly wrought iron and ceramic artefacts, a pastel confusion, the pervasive aroma of quality coffee and baked goods. A civilised place, complete with civilised people, ladies with leisure time, young mums and their babies, grandparents, generations of family and friends seeking distraction from the damp on a late January Tuesday afternoon. Life-sucking claustrophobia, thick as stormcloud.

It's hard to put an age on her. Carefully tended late sixties, early seventies, maybe. Her face pleasantly etched with the rictus smile-lines of a high-octane social life. Grey hair accentuated with high and low tones, make-up a delicate balance of luminescence and emphasis, lipstick matched perfectly to enhance the residual colour of her lips. She moves with grace, the ease of functioning joints, an elegance I envy, underscoring the ragged edges of the past few weeks, writ large on me. My hair needing cut and colour, my skin dry, my eyes exhausted. Every bone aches.

'I'm so glad you could meet me, Ailish,' she says.

I nod. Smile. Unsure what words are required.

'Moira told me the story. What happened after we left.'

'I know.'

'Stupid question, but how are you doing?'

'We're okay. I think.'

Intelligent eyes seep sympathy, bore into me, seek my soul.

'Well, we're adjusting.'

'It must have been hard. Keeping such a secret for so long. And so difficult telling Gerry and the girls.'

Her voice is practised balm, professional do-gooder, dripping with sympathy I'm not looking for.

'You're very brave.'

I stare at her. My best attempt at fuck-you-cool, channel my inner bitch, my inner bad girl.

The word – brave – repulses me.

'They're beautiful children, Saoirse and Róisín,' she continues, undaunted. 'I imagine they're supportive?'

And I'm not sure they are. Supportive. Wokely accepting, maybe? Of the story I've told. Sixteen years old, a drunken one-night stand, a crisis pregnancy, a trip to England. A common tale. All true. Details blurred around the edges. It's a long time ago, after all, and who wants to imagine their mother having sex, a sibling who never lived. I am sure they, as I, would have avoided this known between us. If we'd had a choice. A long-ago tragic tale, burning a hole in the blanket they call home.

'Moira said Gerry was finding it hard at first, but you've agreed to some couples counselling?'

'Yes,' I say.

Feeling small, childish. A miscreant brought to book by the headmistress, shown the error of her ways.

'I think that's a good idea. Look, forgive me. I know I'm interfering. But I'm fond of Moira, and you were so good to us at Christmas and, well ... it's something I have an interest in. There may be some way I can help.'

'To be honest, Jean, I agreed to meet you to please Moira, to please Gerry, but it's really a very private matter. I don't want it on display. This is something that happened to me long before I met Gerry, information I hadn't shared with my family because I really didn't – I really don't – think it's relevant to our lives now.'

'Is that not a bit naive?'

'I'm sorry?'

'I don't mean to be blunt. I'm on your side. But, in my experience, something like this always has a long-term impact on your family's life, whether it's out in the open or not.'

I shake my head. 'I didn't tell anybody because ... all the obvious reasons. I didn't want to be judged. To have my daughters look at me as they're looking at me now. I didn't want them to see me ...'

'As a victim?'

'Well. I don't see myself as a victim. I'm not a victim.'

'Really? If it were Saoirse or Róisín in a similar situation, how would you see it?'

I shrug.

'I get it, Ailish,' Jean says, her face shifting, vulnerable. 'I'm not pulling this from thin air. The word victim seems disempowering. I didn't like it either, when it was me.'

And, shaking slightly, her voice modulated and dignified, Jean proceeds to tell me her story. Which is not the same, its own twists and nuances. But it's not entirely different either.

'So many of us have them,' she says eventually. 'Our stories.'

I nod. Because I can't speak right now.

27

A Child.
   Colourless,
    Shivering,
        silently stitched
     to an unmade bed,
fingernails
     bitten
       to the quick can
        still pluck eyelashes
         lacerate skin in folds
          consume sketchbooks
           in shredded confusion
           disturbed depictions of
           destroyed promise(s)
          eating her from
        the inside
    desperate for
   somebody,
anybody
to take
Pity.

28

Fiona and I meet for dinner in The Green Hen. I'm shocked to realise it must be nearly two years since we've seen each other in person. All the busyness, all the different life stages.

'Sorry, sorry, sorry,' she says.

She's wearing a shapeless black-and-grey jersey dress and looks like she's put on weight. Her roots are half an inch long, the hair itself a new wiry, her make-up imprecise. Her face is calm and happy. When we hug, the years melt in the movement of us, the muscle-memory twitches and tics and intonations of us, only mildly slowed by time.

'Don't lie, you're not a bit sorry,' I say. 'Wine? Bottle?'

'Yes. White?'

We order. Get menus. Ignore the waiter, who is overeager, trying to flirt, pegs us, maybe, as a generous tip.

'How's Rachel? Oh my God, I forgot her Christmas present,' I say.

'She'll hold it against you, that one. She's cute out. But a dote compared to her brothers. Those little fuckers have the house wrecked, my head wrecked, and Mark is only useless.'

'Ah, I remember him being lovely with them.'

'Oh, he's grand when he's playing games, he's a just big child himself. Any sniff of discipline is left to me. I'm not able for it, Ail. I'm too old to have four under-eights. You should have told me this.'

'You wouldn't have listened.'

'You still could have said.'

'You knew – the nuclear family is an outdated social construct, remember?'

'Fuck you.'

We laugh. She looks at the menu. Holds it at arm's length and squints.

'Mum would like to see you,' she says.

'I'll get out to her soon.'

'Yeah, yeah.'

'I will.'

'Do. She's still flying it, y'know. Great advertisement for not having a man around.'

I laugh.

'How did you get on with the Citizen's Assembly wan?' she says.

'Fine.'

'Fine?'

'Fine. She's a nice woman. Has her own crosses. She means well.'

'Uh huh.'

'She does.'

'Yes, but for you or The Cause? Be careful you don't get sucked into something you're not really up for.'

'Like?'

'The debate is going to get heated. The last thing you need is to be some activist group's poster girl.'

'Give me some credit. That wouldn't happen.'

'Not intentionally.'

'She's interested in the debate, putting all sides out there, letting people make up their minds. She wants me to go to some of the assembly sessions. She thinks I might have something to contribute from a legal perspective ...'

'Would you?'

'Not my area of expertise, but I've been following it. Had a personal interest, obviously.'

Fiona shifts, adjusts her dress.

'I can't believe you never told me, Ail. It must have been so lonely for you.'

The waiter comes back, takes our orders.

Fiona stares at me. Intently. Uncomfortably. I squirm.

I want to say 'I wasn't allowed'. Realise how childish this sounds.

'I thought we were so close,' she says.

'We were.'

'But you said nothing. Not once.'

'I didn't tell anybody. Well, I nearly told Niall. He had his own demons. I guess I considered mine bigger. More shameful.'

She shakes her head.

'I wonder what happened to him?'

'Niall? I haven't heard from him in years. Few cards after he went to the States, then nothing.'

And feel sad because I loved Niall. All the people and elements of your life who are so crucial at a particular point in time, then, without warning, they're the past. Doors you can no longer gain access to. A one-way system.

Our food arrives. Her steak, my risotto.

I could have predicted our choices when booking.

29

We sit, lined up like kindergarteners, in front of Dr O'Brien, family GP for decades, age-leeched of pigmentation now, style and swagger somewhat intact. He smiles at us, then nods a considered conspiracy to my father.

'So, Frank. Bit of confusion, they tell me?'

'Ah, it's nothing, nothing at all, Joe. They're making a fuss over nothing. Women.' His best barstool bravura.

'Well, let's prove them wrong then,' Dr O'Brien says. 'I just need to ask you a few questions, if that's okay? Standard stuff. Nothing hard.'

'Well, I'm not telling you what's in the Will, if that's what they're after,' Frank says. 'They can bide their time for that.'

We laugh.

'This is just a precautionary measure, Dad,' I say. 'We'd like to get an Enduring Power of Attorney signed, Dr O'Brien, just in case. You never know what's around the corner. We've all got Dad's best interests at heart.'

'No doubt,' Dr O'Brien says. 'No doubt. Relax there, Frank,

take off your coat. This'll take about twenty minutes or so, best be comfortable. It's just simple a set of questions. First off, can you tell me what date it is today?'

'Well, I'm always very happy to get out of January, so I know it's already turned February. Is it the seventh?'

'It is indeed. And d'you know what time it is?'

'Our appointment was for three, and you're late, so I'd say it's about twenty past.'

'No flies on you, are there?'

'Well, of course he's fine now, but he's been so confused at home,' Barbara says.

She's twitching.

'He put the post in the fridge the other day,' she says.

'Well, I do strange things myself when I'm distracted sometimes,' Dr O'Brien says. 'Would you prefer to wait outside, Barbara? There's no need for all of you to be here.'

'Well ...'

'We'll stay,' I say. 'If that's okay.'

We're out in fifteen minutes. Frank is deemed compos mentis, has agreed to an Enduring Power of Attorney – 'Well, Ailish is a lawyer, isn't she? She'll know what to do.' – and Barbara is not happy.

'Of course, he was fine in there, wasn't he?' she says. 'It's when he's home with me alone that the problems start. I can't cope, Ailish, I won't be able to cope, not with my knee and the operation and everything.'

I'm looking again at getting them home help, but this isn't a popular choice either. Barbara doesn't want someone else in her space – 'I've always been very private,' she says – an oblique reference to the denouement at Christmas? – 'You just don't know what he's going to say next.'

In truth, Frank's lapses are more pronounced by the week. Days when he gets up and gets dressed for work, though it has been years since he left the Civil Service, days when he thinks I still live at home, days when he calls her 'Mammy'. The day he drops the A word again, in passing, and I realise he must have known all along. That it has sat there in his head too. All this time. Is lurching now, straining now, to get out.

'I told Dr O'Brien,' I say. 'When we were leaving, I told him the memory problems are real, I've witnessed them, and I'm worried.'

'Then why doesn't he do something?'

'Do what, Mum? He passed the tests. We have the Enduring Power of Attorney, if and when we need it. We can't do much more than that at the moment.'

'I can't look after him. Not long term. I know you're soft about these things, Ailish, but sooner than later he will need to go into a home.'

'Soft about these things?'

'You know what I mean.'

'No, I don't think I do, Mum. What do you mean?'

'Life is hard, Ailish. Sometimes tough decisions need to be made.'

30

Jean wants me to write my story. She's helping curate a selection of first-hand experiences for the assembly. I've sat in on the debate, listened to some of the speakers, the so-called ordinary citizens in the room, complex positions put forward by expert thinkers, terms like 'moral status', 'care pathways', 'autonomy', the emotive buzz, and all the while my brain, my body, is overwhelmed, thoughts and feelings reflecting and refracting round my head like gunshot in a sniper's alley.

At a remove, Gerry is supportive. We have reference and language for this now, in the New Ireland.

'I'm not sure how I feel about it, Ailish,' Gerry says. 'But, of course, if you think it will help you get closure, then you should do it.'

'I think you should too, Mum,' says Saoirse.

Róisín is quieter.

Lots of hugs.

But the words don't appear easily on the page. And when they do, they are clunky, guilty, full of shame. Wrong. Clashing in my head with easily justifiable narratives of foetal abnormalities, rape, clinical necessity.

Gerry reads a first draft.

'I know I said I wouldn't,' he says. 'But ...'

'I only met him a few times,' I say. 'He's not relevant. He never even knew.'

'He's not walking around Dublin now, is he? I wouldn't know him?'

'Oh, for God's sake, Gerry, don't make this about you.'

'I'm not *making* it about me. Fuck it, it *is* about me. It's not the fact of it, or him, whoever he is, it's the fact of the secret. That you never told me.'

'How much counselling do we need to do? I didn't tell anybody. Not even Fiona, or Niall. I shared it with nobody. You weren't special.'

It hangs. Smells. Permeates.

'Your husband wasn't special?' he says.

'I didn't want to hurt you,' I say. 'I don't want to hurt anybody. Don't you understand? I wanted to forget it ever happened. Pretend it was only a clump of cells, a late period. That it meant nothing. I didn't want to think about its due date, whether it would have been a boy or a girl, how old it would be every year, who it would look like ... And I do. I think about it all the time, even now. When I look at the girls. It wasn't an easy decision. And it wasn't even my decision.'

'I know it can't have been easy for you. I get that. But you must see how this has blindsided me? It's a big thing to have between us. I feel, I don't know, like it redefines everything.'

'Redefines everything? Are you saying you don't keep secrets from me? You've always been one hundred percent honest and transparent?'

'Yes, of course I have.'

'Really? I'd think carefully before you say that.'

'I don't know what you mean.'

'What about – for example – Viva?'

'Viva?'

'You fucking hypocrite, Gerry. Joe organised an abortion for that girl and you helped him.'

'I helped her.'

'What do you mean, you helped her?'

'What I said. The girl was distraught. I helped her. You threw her out.'

* * *

Moira gets wind from Jean that the personal experiences are to be recorded, to be broadcast, put on the internet. Gets wind from Gerry that I've been considering it.

'You'd get an actress or someone to read it, though, wouldn't you? You couldn't read it yourself, people would recognise your voice,' she says.

'I think it would almost be my duty to read it myself, Moira. Your friend Jean, she's all about authenticity.'

Her face. Worth it.

* * *

A hard edge in the house you could cut. More brittle and passive-aggressive than the smack-bang cold surfaces. Gerry and I pass each other on the stairs without words. He sleeps in the spare room, a fact the girls don't acknowledge. They are buried in past exam papers, spend spare time in grinds, support each other with swotting in a way that would be cute if I didn't suspect it to be riven by anxiety, insecurity, all the emotions I hoped to spare them.

* * *

I cook, wash their clothes, clean their rooms on the sly. Try to fade into the background.

'I'm sorry, Jean,' I say. 'I can't. It's not just about me.'

She understands.

31

Barbara's knee operation is a semi-success. The new joint is in and, according to the physio, functioning, but there's tear damage to the meniscus which may take time to heal, a small chance it never will. A bed is brought down to the living room, meals served on a tray, personal hygiene reduced to complicated negotiations with a facecloth and towel in the downstairs loo.

She won't hear of a nurse, wanted me to move in completely for the duration. We've compromised on two weeknights and weekends. I've taken time off work, left the girls to their own devices and our home help, and I've nothing left in any tank. When I'm not doing her shopping, cleaning, filling prescriptions or organising meals, I'm trying to maintain order on Frank, who is disintegrating further by the day, going quieter, aware of large gaps in his own cognition, afraid of embarrassing himself. Afraid of my mother, spread wide on the bed, immobility and a taste for pasta converging in inflated skin bare to brushed cotton, the sight of her mutated form, my new intimacy with it, disturbing on a visceral level.

Her need for control is terrifying. Palpable. Endless lists. Capital letters, underlined, torn pages and reused envelopes, catalogues from Lidl and Aldi, items she does and doesn't need, ringed in red. Relentless picking. Frank a source of constant irritation, derision. Any small weakness called out – 'It's Ailish, Frank, do you not remember your own daughter?' – and imbued with sinister meaning. A sly nod to me, evidence amassing to support her bid to tidy him away, preserve some increasingly fragile veneer of respectability, this phantom portrait of her life.

I swing between two worlds, a link between my daughters and my mother, from colour and light and hope to this musty past life, the remnants of it clung to me like the smell of soured milk. And all the while I watch my parents' sticky decline, a question swirling in my head. Growing. How did Frank know about the Trip to England? Did he guess? Did she tell him? How? When?

I try to broach it but, even now, as I approach my own half-century, a mother myself of girls older than I was then, it's not a topic I can raise without feeling like a child displaying a prurient interest in adult things that don't concern her. Deserving of the inevitable brush-off. Helping her awkwardly from commode to bed one day I try, simply.

'Did you tell him?'

and am rewarded with a breathy

'Sure didn't I have to tell somebody?'

32

27 May 2018: 6.31am

The phone rings.

'Mum, Mum, we won!'

The referendum results are confirmed. Róisín is on holidays in Greece with friends. I suspect a boyfriend, but we won't have that conversation yet. Saoirse is … I'm not sure where.

I'm still in bed. Groggy and tired from the campaign. Backroom stuff. Jean has been keeping me busy.

I can't answer the child.

I weep.

6.50am

The phone rings.

I've made my way to the kitchen. Have flicked a switch on the kettle.

'Ailish? This is Marie, from Aldridge. I'm so sorry, Ailish ...'

I drop my mug onto the porcelain-tiled floor.

It shatters. Powdery shards. Tiny, tiny particles of dust.

33

The Church: familiar, like home. Home from home. Pillars, pews, tabernacle. Red carpet.

Me: aged four, running onto the altar, veined white marble and the red-velvet cushion on the priest's chair smooth on scratched bare legs before my mother snatches me away.

Me: today, tidy in a new black coat, belted, contained. Face made and set. Catching an eye, swerving an eye, accepting sympathy in semi-smiles. How should one arrange one's features? Will a badly timed twitch or tilt betray an inappropriate feeling? What is an appropriate feeling? How to perform grief to the satisfaction of watchers.

Them (aloud): 'Sorry for your troubles.' Shake my hand. File by. Again. And again. Faces I haven't seen for decades. Skin worn and collapsing in preordained folds.

Them (hushed): 'She didn't last long in the end.' 'They don't, do they, when they go into a home?' 'Sure she didn't have any choice.' 'It's hard to mind an invalid.' 'Poor Barbara. She didn't deserve that.'

Brendan and Elena: sombre. Solid. Adept at funerals now. Walking the aisle like sad penguins. Forever a pair.

The Cousins: their grown children. How strange to see the parents' familiar faces reflected, reshaped, reformed. Louisa's daughters linked by their colouring. Black hair, perfect skin, those dark-well eyes. The oldest one is heavy-featured, like her father. A curl of dissatisfaction hovering along her lip. Like her mother. The youngest one has a little girl of her own now. Louisa is a granny.

Joe: and his five sons. Lined up like skittles in black suits around Helen, puffy with ill health. Her kidneys failing, they say.

Sarah: poised, her face pitched perfectly. Sympathy. Empathy. Understanding. A lifetime of making the best of things.

Michael: *Oh, Michael. Oh.* Didn't expect that. Still a boy. The curve of his head. Flashback, twelve-year-old me, Granny's funeral in the kitchen. Everything changed now. Or has it? Is that a small flutter? Of what? Sliding doors. Closed. But. I caught a glimpse.

Ciarán: the awkward length of him sloping near the bier, spade-like hands suspended unsure in the air. Not right. Never right. No diagnosis. Too many diagnoses.

Gerry: in charge, comfortable with the people. Swinging his shirt-strained gut as if it is not part of him. This is what middle-aged men are made of, sandwiches and soup and Guinness acquired at funerals.

My Girls: beautiful. Their father's daughters, working the room. A family largely unknown to them now, a tenuous tether to an alien tribe. Delicate features against their cousins' heavyset bulk.

Frank: my father. Dad. Daddy. Still handsome. Still lost. Wandering corridors of his memory now in vague bemusement.

'Your mother?' he says.

Pointing to the coffin.

I nod.

He shakes his head.

'A difficult woman.'

'When you think about your mother now, what comes to mind first?'

The words are important. You feel their weight. Measure them.

'She had it hard,' you say.

'How so?

'To be a girl, a woman, in that time. It was hard.'

'It was a difficult era for women. No more than your own.'

'But she had so little independence. So few choices. She had to give up her job when she married Frank, you know. That was how it was, then. And she couldn't have children.'

'She had you.'

'She had me.'

You smooth an invisible crease on your skirt.

'It's the thought of her loneliness that gets me,' you say.

Evenly, with effort.

The woman nods.

'And you? Are you not lonely?'

Breathe.

'I have more choices,' you say. 'I can manage independently, if I want to. I'm in the world, I can seek out a tribe. I'm really not so worried about what 'they' think. That's what I've been thinking. She was hemmed in by her upbringing, her husband, her social status. Financially.'

'Sounds like you've decided to give her a bit of a let.'

'Maybe I'm also just deciding not to guilt myself for my own shortcomings.'

The woman nods.

'Sounds like a good choice.'

You laugh.

'If you'd had a choice,' the woman says, 'back in 1985, how do you think you would have chosen?'

You lean forward. Shake your head.

Inhale.

'I wouldn't have chosen to have a baby at sixteen.'

The woman nods, slowly.

'So you've found peace with it?'

'Do we ever really find peace?'

'Maybe not.'

'I'm more resolved – or resigned – to it. To my experience, I guess.'

'Good.'

You look at the clock on the table. Five to the hour. Smile.

'Nearly time,' you say.

'Shall I book you in for next week?'

'Can I give you a call?'
'Sure.'

You pick up your coat, and your bag, a graceful movement
which shifts the light in the space,

and as you leave with a small wave,

your face is

flooded with light, a sudden smile

a ghost of the girl you were at sixteen

all the women you have been in between

271

the woman you might become

                              a fluid continuum of movement

until all that's left is an imprint of perfume on air

              a click of the front door, heels on cobbles.

Acknowledgements

Apologies in advance. This is going to be one of those gratuitously long acknowledgements because this book simply would not have happened without a groundswell of good will and good people in my life. I am so grateful to you all. And apologies if I've left anybody out!

At the beginning (writing wise) – thanks to Veronica Casey who gave me a thorough grounding in the basics when I rocked up in her creative writing class in Cabinteely Community School in 2012. I am proud to call you my friend, along with Hugh McCormack and John Field, whom I met in those classes. You have all played a huge part in keeping me sane over the past few years.

Thanks also to Hugh, for introducing me to Ferdia Mac Anna and his workshops, initially in Dalkey, on Zoom throughout the pandemic, and latterly in the fabulous Books Upstairs. I hold Ferdia solely responsible for giving me NOTIONS – none of this would have happened without the confidence he so quietly and expertly gifts his students. He also introduced me to my writing tribe – Seymour Cresswell, now my Poolbeg partner-incrime (who would have thunk it!), the incredible 'Scribble Sisters' – Cathy Power, Lucina Russell, Jenny Langley, Deirdre Miller and Dorothée Kuepers – also Zan Sinnott, Denise Tormey, Fionnuala Sweeney, Sarah Myers, Seán Duke, Catherine Daly, the inimitable Kay Holliday, and many more who have helped me while away happy and creative Saturday mornings.

The thing with Notions is they have a tendency to take flight. In September 2021, mine led me to the Creative Writing Masters in University of Limerick. They found a home and were nurtured there by the wonderful faculty: Joseph O'Connor, Donal Ryan, Sarah Moore Fitzgerald, Emily Cullen, Eoin Deveraux, Yianna Liatsos. I am forever grateful for your encouragement and advice and to the extended writing tribe I found there including and especially: Máirín Stronge, Natalie Robinson, Sarah Lou Ryan, Geraldine O'Sullivan, Anna Ryan Maloney, Seán Coffey, Elaine Kiely, Bob McDonald, Conor Clohessy, Neil Tully, Barbara Kavanagh, Jane Babb, all the rest of ye who suffered drafts and gave input on *Ailish* in workshops.

Thank you also and especially to:

Jenny Langley, Seán Coffey, Nuala Deering and Lorraine Lowe who read early full drafts.

Asta O'Sullivan, Conasta, for her creative photography.

Paula Campbell and Kieran Devlin in Poolbeg for deciding to publish.

Gaye Shortland, editor and emoji-expert, huge extra special thanks for bearing with me when I wobbled.

David Prendergast for all the wobbles I (inadvertently) caused him with the typesetting.

My bookclub (nothing like the one depicted in this book!) Jackie Borza, Ciara Holmes, Rosemary Kelly, Ailish Langan, Linda Farren and Nikki Lee – and the legendary women in my life it seems I can always rely on: Deirdre Matthews, Martina Keane, Thelma Cowley, Eve Cluskey, Fionnuala Downes, Lorraine Lowe, Muireann Stack, Sarah Maguire, Emma Clancy, Helen Caffrey, Martina O'Kane, Celine Creighton, Ciara McDermott, Jennifer Sealy, Sinéad Martin and Arlene Sommerville – for suffering me, and providing 'focus group' advice.

My Menarini work colleagues, especially those in the Dublin office, in particular Angela Gillian and Francis Lynch, for their patience, facilitation and encouragement of The Notions.

My Wexford family – Andrew & Claire Paul, Simon & Lucia Watson.

My sisters, Gillian and Geraldine, brothers-in-law, Adam and Richie, nieces Lucy, Morgan, Ellen and nephew Ruairí. The Guard family – Kristian, Sioned, Joss, Felicity, Rich, Lia, Owen, Cara and William.

Flynn Ashton and Victoria Kerins O'Brien, for their unending support during tough times and for being lovely.

Foremost and finally, thanks to Alex and Emma, two amazing humans who are my everything,